Praise for

Mastered

Well written and insanely hot... One of the things I liked best about this book was the way Cartwright had of explaining the BDSM lifestyle... I'm definitely looking forward to the next installment in this Mastered series and will be rereading With This Collar while I wait, for it is a great scorching love story well worth reading at any time. ~ *Whipped Cream*

This very spicy read gives a beautiful exposition of one woman's journey into an erotic world that she knew very little of... There are very hot scenes that demonstrate some of the techniques that can be applied but this is also a delicious love story and I look forward to reading more titles from this gifted author. ~ *Night Owl Romance*

Ms. Cartwright managed to deliver yet another amazing BDSM story. I enjoyed reading With this Collar immensely. It is well written and perfectly paced. The characters are great—even the side ones that I can't wait to read more about—and there are just enough witty lines to highlight the sassy part of their personalities... Can't wait to read more.
~ *The Romance Reviews*

With This Collar by Sierra Cartwright is a beautifully written BDSM story that contains the heart and soul of the BDSM world. Ms. Cartwright did not miss a beat in creating Master Marcus and Julia... As far as the plot goes, this is a rock solid read that will heat you up in a Nano second! The characters demand your attention as the story unfolds. I enjoyed the fact that Julia fights back. What can I say...I like a woman with gumption. *LOL!* Ms. Cartwright is a master in her own right when it comes to writing the BDSM genre. She gets an A++ from me. With This Collar is a must have for anyone's BDSM collection. Bring on the next book in the series! ~ *BlackRaven's Reviews*

Mastered

OVER THE LINE

SIERRA CARTWRIGHT

Over the Line
ISBN # 978-1-78184-619-3
©Copyright Sierra Cartwright 2013
Cover Art by Posh Gosh ©Copyright May 2013
Interior text design by Claire Siemaszkiewicz
Total-E-Bound Publishing

Published in 2013 by Total-E-Bound Publishing, Think Tank, Ruston Way, Lincoln, LN6 7FL, United Kingdom.

Total-E-Bound Publishing is an imprint of Total-E-Ntwined Limited.

OVER THE LINE

Dedication

For Total-E-Bound — you all are fabulous!
To the Pineapple Gang — Scarlett, Goldi, Lexy, Mel.
And for some fun, new fabu friends — Jean, Leslie,
Carolyn, Shelley, Laurie, Leaundra and Susan — you
help keep me sane. Either that, or you're such good
friends, you join me on my journey!
Don — always and all ways…

Chapter One

Michael Dayton caught a whiff of spiced vanilla, and he turned his head to find the source.

The view of the woman passing by walloped him. He only managed a brief look at her face, not enough to make out her eye colour, but on a primal level he noted the softness of her mouth and the sexy gloss that accented her lips.

She kept moving in the direction of the fire pit. And like the male that he was, he didn't look away. How could he? She was tiny, compact, with blonde hair tumbling over her shoulders, the strands an untamed riotous mass. She walked with determination, her hips swaying seductively as she navigated the uneven flagstone patio. Her grace was even more remarkable given the unyielding leather dress and her crazy-high stilettos. Even though the shoes added extra height, she didn't look tall. In fact, he doubted she'd reach his chin.

A need to protect flared in him. The sensation was as unexpected as it was unwelcome.

On occasion, he played with women at Damien's home, known as the Den. Michael had been sexually attracted to many of them. But he'd only had this kind of visceral reaction one other time in his thirty years. He'd ignored his intuition and the warnings of others and had ended up married within three months.

A few years later, he and his bride had been in court, and he'd spent most of his inheritance to hold onto the Eagle's Bend Ranch. The two thousand acres had been in his family for over eighty years, and if he had lost it, he was certain his father would haunt him from the grave. The lessons Michael had learnt while rebuilding his life and fortune had made him harder, smarter and more wary.

He adjusted his cowboy hat and continued to look at the blonde. She had joined a group of people near the fire. Her figure-hugging dress did as much to arouse him as nudity would have.

Until this moment, he hadn't missed having a woman in his bedroom, tied to his rustic four-poster bed, arms and legs spread wide as she lay there for him, willing and waiting. Last night he'd gone to bed alone after masturbating to ease the day's tension. Tonight, he hoped things would be different. He was glad he hadn't simply tossed away the invitation to the Den's solstice party. Although, he admitted, if he took this woman home, he'd wish for a longer night rather than a longer day.

As if sensing his perusal, she glanced over her shoulder. They made eye contact for less than five seconds, but it was enough, more than enough for him.

He heard someone say, "She's trouble."

Michael blinked and reluctantly turned towards the newcomer, Gregorio, the Den's caretaker.

"Don't go there," Gregorio advised, coming to a stop in front of him.

But Michael was already thinking about her, despite the fact she didn't resemble the women who generally caught his eye. He preferred a more rounded, feminine form—a woman who could withstand the rigours of ranch life.

"Her name's Sydney Wallace," Gregorio said.

Michael was aware of Gregorio's voice, but his focus was elsewhere. Sydney. Unusual name. He let it roll around in his mind, imagined how it might sound when he said it aloud as he told her what to do.

"She used to dance nude in a cabaret in Vegas and has a boa constrictor as a pet. It killed her last Dom and dragged him out to the backyard. She's on the run from the law. We heard she's wanted in ten states and two Canadian provinces." Gregorio snapped his fingers near Michael's face, jarring him from his reverie. "You listening to me, Mike?"

"Huh?" He shook his head and looked at Gregorio.

"I figured you weren't listening, otherwise you'd have decked me for calling you Mike." Gregorio chuckled. "Seriously, if you want to play, there are a number of subs here tonight—they're wearing the house's purple wrist band. That means they're available for a scene, they know the rules and they follow them. Any one of them would be much better for you than Sydney."

Gregorio, as Damien Lowell's right-hand man, knew things. Gregorio understood human nature and, since he tracked all the membership applications, he had insider knowledge of everyone at the Den. He served as a house monitor and sometimes participated in scenes. Because he was so well respected, Doms and subs alike listened to him. Those who didn't often rued their decision.

For the first time, Michael wanted to ignore Gregorio's unsolicited advice. "I didn't see a collar around her neck." He took in the people she was standing with. "And she doesn't seem to be here with anyone."

"She doesn't have a Dom."

"I'll bite. What's wrong with Ms Wallace?"

"Other than the snake and the problems with the law?"

"What?" he asked, taking a drink of the light beer from his cup and looking back at her. A waiter approached with a tray full of sparkling water, and she snagged a flute. Her back was to him, and he couldn't drag his gaze away from her shapely derrière. "Is she a Domme?"

"She's a sub," Gregorio said, giving the answer Michael wanted. "But one with no real interest in a relationship with a man."

He blinked. "She's gay?" Please God, no, not now that he was imagining her legs wrapped around his waist as he drove into her wet pussy.

"She likes men just fine. What I mean is, she'll start playing, if a guy interests her. If he bores her, she bails."

"She'll leave in the middle of a scene?"

"It's happened a handful of times." Gregorio folded his arms across his chest. "She's earned the name 'The Brat' around here."

"She sounds like a challenge," Michael said.

Gregorio laughed. The sound was both ominous and sympathetic. "A few other Doms have felt the same way," Gregorio said. "Sydney has a history of battering hearts and egos."

Water in hand, she walked around to the far side of the fire pit and stood there alone. He responded to the unspoken cue. After finishing his beer in a single gulp, he handed the empty glass to Gregorio. "Wish me luck."

Gregorio grinned. "You'll need more than luck, my friend."

Michael moved towards the fire pit.

Perhaps hearing his approach, she looked up and waited for him.

"Evening, ma'am," he said, as he stopped near her.

"I was hoping you would be brave enough to come and talk to me," she said with a smile that could roll his socks down. "I saw you talking with Gregorio. No doubt he tried to frighten you away with tales of how terrible I am."

"And are you?"

"I suppose there could be some truth to it." She shrugged easily. "But there's not. A good story is always better than the truth."

She smelt potently dangerous. The vanilla was mixed with unadulterated pheromones, and it was a cocktail he couldn't get enough of. "Either way, not much scares me."

"A man among men."

"Michael Dayton. Master Michael." Although the June sun hadn't completely vanished behind the distant mountain peaks, torches were being lit, adding to the ambience and catching streaks of red in her hair. He wanted to touch those strands, to curl them around his fist as he held her down and made her scream.

"Sydney Wallace," she said, returning the formality.

"May I call you Sydney?"

She rolled her glass between her palms. With a tease in her voice, she said, "I'm hoping you can be considerably more creative than that."

He tipped back the brim of his hat to get a better look at her. She intrigued him. "So name calling is not on your limits list."

A server, this one a woman in a French maid's outfit that left nothing to the imagination, walked nearby. Though she was curvy with luscious bare breasts, he only had eyes for the woman he was with.

Sydney placed her glass on the tray. He appreciated the fact that she didn't need something to toy with.

When they were alone again, she said, "I understand you're divorced, Mr Dayton. No kids. You have a ranch you'd like to protect from gold-diggers. You scene every once in a while, and you're not looking for a serious commitment."

"Do you know my blood type?"

She gave a quick grin. "No. I only asked about the important stuff."

"You found out a lot quickly."

"I like being prepared. If I'm going to spend an hour with a man, I want to make sure the time is worth it. I don't think it's fair to either of us if there are false expectations."

"You're mistaken, Sydney."

"About which part?"

"We'll be spending more than an hour together. I can't get you properly warmed up in under sixty minutes, and I intend to keep you on the edge, writhing for an orgasm for much, much longer than that."

Her eyes widened, and for the first time he noticed how blue they were, a shade of ice, a shocking contradiction to the heat she radiated.

"That's a brash statement, Michael."

He captured her chin gently. "Find out for yourself, Ms Wallace. Let's have an experiment here at the Den to see if we have chemistry. After that, we can head out to my ranch. It's about forty-five minutes from here. Or if you'd prefer, we can go to your place. Wherever you feel most comfortable." He noticed her legs were alluringly bare. He'd always been a stockings man. Or at least he had been. Until now. "Are you wearing underwear?"

"I…"

With his index finger, he stroked her cheekbone. "I asked you a question."

"Yes."

"What kind?"

She hesitated for a moment, and he wondered if she was going to answer or whether she was going to run. He held her lightly enough that her movements weren't restricted.

"Boy shorts," she said.

"Please remove them for me."

"Now? Here?"

"Maybe you're the one who should be afraid," he said quietly, "rather than me. Gregorio says you often bail out of scenes. I wondered at first if it was because Doms asked too much from you. But I'm thinking they probably don't ask enough. I've known you less than five minutes, but I've figured out you're assertive. You know what you want, but I'm guessing you're not always good at asking for it. Furthermore," he added, leaning closer towards her, "I'm willing to bet you're bored with anyone who isn't as aggressive as you are. Am I wrong about that?"

She shivered. Since the Colorado evening was mild and they were standing near the fire, he knew she couldn't be cold. So something he'd said had hit a nerve.

Surprising him, she unflinchingly met his gaze. "You're right about the fact I get bored easily," she admitted. She put her hand around his wrist. "And you're wrong if you think I'm afraid of anything."

"Fair enough. In that case, take off your panties." He released his grip on her chin and she let go of him. He stayed in place, physically and figuratively refusing to give her space.

He offered his arm and she held onto it while precariously balancing on her heels.

Finally, she straightened and looked at him as she dangled the pretty pink material from her index finger. Too late he realised he'd made a mistake by not asking to see them on her first. The material had probably stretched across her derrière, highlighting her butt cheeks perfectly.

He accepted the proffered underwear and stuffed the lace and nylon confection in his pocket. Who would have suspected that she wore something so pretty beneath black leather? "What are your limits?"

"I haven't found any," she said.

"Then you've been playing with the wrong Doms."

She shrugged. "That's possible. But maybe I'm tougher than you think."

"Perhaps," he agreed, but with some scepticism. His ex-wife had let him believe she wanted things raw, but the moment the ring had been placed on her finger, the figurative collar had come off her throat. "Humiliation?"

"I don't have a lot of experience with that."

"No one has made you stand in a corner with your nose pressed to the wall when you misbehaved?"

She stiffened. Michael figured he'd hit a nerve. Then the moment passed. Her lips parted for a moment, just long enough for him to wonder how she tasted. He loved anticipation, enjoyed getting a woman so turned on she lost her inhibitions, but now, with Sydney, unaccustomed impatience nipped at him.

"I don't misbehave," she said with an impish grin.

He raised his eyebrows. "Never? Or have you not played with a Dom long enough to establish a relationship?"

She gave a soft sigh. "Would you like to psychoanalyse me, Michael? If so, can we sit down somewhere? But honestly, I'm not sure if I'll ever see you again, so I'd prefer we spend an enjoyable evening together."

"I don't rush. I just want to know you a bit better before we play together. I want to give you what you need, not just what you want."

"That's an interesting distinction."

"You might want wine, but need water," he said. "I want you completely satisfied."

"You're right. I kind of move from Dom to Dom," she said. "A man, any man, would complicate my lifestyle. Maybe you think that's selfish, but it's who I am. I was hoping that since you're a divorced man who doesn't want to go through another divorce, you'd be fine with a one-night stand."

"Ouch," he said. When she opened her lovely mouth to speak again, he held up a hand to silence her. To her credit, she shut up. "No, you don't have to watch your words. In fact, I prefer your honesty."

"Really?"

He nodded. "And I'm not against a relationship. I'm not, in theory, against marriage." Passing the land to his heirs would be nice. He had one sister, who had two girls. Despite the fact that he had a couple of horses, none of his relatives had shown any interest in the ranch.

"Are you looking for something permanent now?"

"No," he said.

"Then if you'd like to play, I would, too." Seductively, sexily, she placed her palm over his crotch.

Heat seared through the denim. Except for lovers he'd been with a long time, no woman had been so bold. He wanted to cave to his baser instincts and take her here, now. Instead, he captured her hand and moved it away.

She pulled back, breaking his grip, and he knew she felt rejected. What man in his right mind would have stopped her? "Don't take it personally," he said. "Please. I will want you to do that in the future, and right now I want to be buried balls-deep in your hot cunt as you cry out my name."

Her eyes opened wide. She seemed more intrigued than shocked. "I want that, too," she admitted.

"We need to clear up a few things."

"Right. I have no STDs, I have no physical limitations. Oh, yes, and I have condoms in my purse—large. And medium, just in case." She grinned. "I've been called an eternal optimist. I don't need that size as much as most men would have you believe."

He shook his head. The charming Ms Wallace was trying to goad him, and he appreciated her efforts. Rather than responding, he changed the subject, "Why do you scene?"

"Why?"

"You've thought about it, surely?"

"I guess I'm always wondering where my limits are, and I like to transcend them. I mountain climb. White water river raft. I did a triathlon, and I'm competing in an upcoming mud race, you know, running up a mountain then doing obstacle courses, under barbed wire, over a wooden wall. My team is doing it for charity."

He was forced to look at her more objectively. His initial urge had been to care for her. Now he wondered if she could kick his ass. Maybe Gregorio had been right to issue warnings. "What's your safe word?"

"Everest."

Of course it was.

"You don't need to know why."

"Okay." He figured he already knew, but he looked forward to her telling him tomorrow morning over coffee. "How about a code for slowing down?"

"I don't believe in that."

"In that case, we'll use the word caution."

She sighed. "If I have to have one, how about we use the word turtle?"

He thumbed his hat. "I think I've just been insulted."

"Not at all. That would be rude. I'm just saying that turtles are slow."

Not only was she attractive, but quick-witted and intelligent. It had been a long time since a woman had appealed to him on multiple levels. "How do you feel about public play?"

She hesitated for a second. "I've never tried it."

"Are you willing to?"

"I suppose."

"I prefer a yes or no answer," he told her. "Unless you'd rather talk about it?"

"No. I mean yes."

"Yes, Sir."

"Yes, Sir," she dutifully repeated.

"Good girl."

He saw her grit her teeth, but she said nothing. He'd hit a nerve demanding she conform to the smallest of courtesies, and he'd remember that. "Do you like impact play?"

Before he could ask further questions, she said, "I find an open-handed spanking to be really pleasurable. I also like belts." She glanced at his waist.

Oh, yeah. He'd happily lay the leather across her rear.

She was quiet for a moment, maybe as discombobulated as he was. And he realised she had an air of vulnerability that she tried to hide. Others probably missed it, but he was glad he hadn't.

"I'm also fine with a shoe or a ruler," she said, her words a hurried rush as if she were attempting to cover the uncomfortable silence. "Anything, really. Feel free to be creative. I'm okay with a flogger, open to trying a bull whip and cane. There isn't a position I'm averse to, over the knee, or a table, or a bed. Standing, kneeling over a spanking bench. Did I miss anything?"

"The Sir at the end of the sentence."

"Of course. Sir." She gave him another of her sunny smiles.

No wonder she ate other Doms for breakfast. She seemed so guileless, he'd bet it would be difficult for some men to hold her accountable. "Clamps?"

She nodded. "The harder the better. As you're probably gathering, I find it easier to get off when there's erotic pain involved."

"Anal plugs?"

She fidgeted then said, "If you insisted, I'd try it."

"No one has claimed your ass?" he asked, stunned.

"No."

That he would be the first to place something up there made him even harder, and his erection pressed against his jeans. He wanted to readjust his cock, but he reminded himself to focus on her. There were a few other things he needed to know before they got started. "Handcuffs?"

"Any kind of bondage," she said.

"I've haven't lassoed a woman." He paused. "Yet."

Her eyes widened. "Sounds interesting."

Michael was suddenly glad he'd ignored Gregorio's advice. The thought of dragging a helpless Sydney towards him was a thrill. If she were barefoot and naked, it would be all the better. "And actual sexual penetration?"

"Like I said, I have condoms. In assorted sizes. I have nothing communicable, I'm on the pill. Anything else you need to know?"

"That will cover it," he said wryly. "Likewise, I have a clean bill of health, but I also believe in covering all the bases. We'll use condoms."

When he said nothing else, she gave a little flip of her hair and turned away, heading towards the house.

"Where are you going, Sydney?"

She stopped and looked over her shoulder. With a puzzled frown, she said, "Inside." She moistened her lips quickly then added, "I thought that was what you wanted."

"Did I say so?"

"No." She returned to stand in front of him. "I apologise."

"I'm going to spank you over there." He nodded towards a short metal fence in the distance. It bordered the grassy area beyond the horseshoe pits, far enough that they'd have some privacy. Still, since it was lit by a number of solar lights and torches, anyone who wanted to watch could.

She glanced around, and he waited patiently.

At least a dozen people were outside, a small group gathered on one side of the fire pit. Some stood around high tables. Elsewhere, a woman sat on a porch swing while her male sub licked her boot.

Another evening at the Den. "I think you need reminding that I prefer to be addressed as Master Michael and Sir. When we play together, Sydney, I make the rules. I will be sure you understand them and agree with them, but once that happens, they will be enforced. Do you understand?"

"Yes, Sir," she whispered.

"Do you agree to address me the way I prefer?"

She nodded.

"Please pull your dress up to your waist."

She couldn't have taken more time. He didn't complain, though. Watching her was its own reward. She was softness and sensuality all wrapped within a woman who was temporarily his.

"Ah," he said when she was exposed. "Such a pretty little pussy. I like that it's shaved." He looked at her expectantly.

"Thank you, Sir."

Interesting—since he'd drawn harsher boundaries, she seemed softer, more compliant. Everything she said and did seemed to be a contradiction. "Please put your hands behind your neck and bring your chest forward."

She did. "Would you like me to take the dress off entirely, Sir?"

"I'd like you to do as you're told, Sydney. Nothing more. Are you able to comfortably spread your legs a little farther apart? You can take off your shoes if you need to."

When she was in position, more open, he slid a hand between her legs. Her response delighted him. "You're moist, Sydney."

He kept his hand still, but she moved her hips a bit, sliding herself against him. "I generally won't mind if you come without permission. In fact, the more you orgasm, the more I get into the scene," he said. "But not tonight. Tonight I want you more aroused than you've ever been." He waited until she let out a tiny moan then he pulled his hand away. Before she could react, he slapped her cunt, hard.

She screamed and pitched forward slightly. He caught her and held her against him longer than necessary, liking the way they fitted together.

For a moment, she stayed there before drawing in a deep breath and moving away. "*That* was unexpected. And unbelievably hot, Sir."

"Turtle?"

"No. More like that, please."

"Stay where you are. I'll be right back."

He went inside. Brandy, a sub who regularly helped with house functions and parties, fetched him a blanket and two separate cuffs.

"My pleasure, Sir," she said when he thanked her.

When he got back outside, Sydney was still in the same place. She was shifting from side to side a bit nervously, but she'd yet to bail out of the scene. "Are you doing okay?"

"Feeling a little exposed," she admitted. "Sir."

"Seeing you when I came back outside pleased me."

She visibly exhaled.

"Would you like to continue?"

"Yes, Sir. I'm not scared," she said, but her voice didn't sound as sure as it had earlier.

He nodded. "In that case, when you're ready, walk over to the fence." Then he scowled. "Are you okay in those shoes?"

"Completely."

"Good. I'll stay a step or two behind you so I can watch your ass move."

The view was all he'd hoped for. There was grace and sultry elegance in her every step. But when she reached the edge of the paved patio, he took her elbow. He helped her over the uneven terrain then draped the blanket over the rail.

Without being told, she kicked off her shoes and positioned herself, even remembering to spread her legs wide. No doubt this was a woman who knew what she wanted. And, whether or not she recognised it, by having her beautifully curved ass upturned and waiting for his attention, she was already giving him what he wanted.

"Use your safe word if it's too much, your slow word if you're uncomfortable or get a muscle cramp. We can get you readjusted."

"Yes, I understand."

"Your choice—I can secure your legs in place or I can cuff your wrists."

She answered unhesitatingly. "I'd prefer you fasten my ankles so I can't get away, Sir."

"I'll expect you to keep your hands wrapped around the bars."

"Yes, of course, Sir."

He crouched to attach the cuffs, and he inhaled the heady scent of her muskiness. Keeping her turned on without letting her come was going to be exquisite. To test the bonds, he trailed his fingers up the insides of her thighs. She squirmed and pulled and yet she helplessly remained where he wanted her. Sometime in the future, he'd stick a plug up her ass too, to intensify her sensations. "I'm going to warm you up with a few spanks," he informed her. "Then I'll make you beg for more."

"You sound sure of yourself, Sir," she said, her voice muffled.

"I am, Sydney."

"You know, Sir, I have never begged for anything my entire life."

"And you've never been spanked by me."

Chapter Two

At Master Michael's confident, arrogant-sounding statement, a thrill that had nothing to do with the bite of evening air arced down Sydney's spine. She had begged before, but not because she had meant it, only because it had been required by the Dom.

But if he could truly drive her that far out of her mind...

She'd fantasised about playing with a Dom who was in tune with her, able to read what she wanted and needed and not just what she asked for.

Her visits to the Den were getting further apart, more from restlessness than because of her schedule. When she travelled, she checked out the scene in whatever city she was visiting. She'd tried new Doms, from seasoned professionals to enthusiastic newbies. And she'd rarely bared herself to the same man twice. She knew her reputation was tarnished, and recently she'd begun to wonder if something was wrong with her.

Like her parents before her, she was a bit of a thrill-seeker. Her first encounter with BDSM at a college party had immediately captured her interest. After that, going back to normal sex hadn't been a possibility. Still, every new high had left her wondering if there was anything else, anything better.

She'd been with some extreme players, and several years ago, she'd knelt to accept a collar. But true affection had been missing between her and Lewis. Finally, things had deteriorated to the point where she'd had a jeweller cut the silver band off her neck. She'd left the pieces in the middle of the bed and never looked back.

On the other hand, Doms who were overly solicitous, as Master Michael had surmised, bored her.

So far, he seemed different from other men. She'd thought that would be a good thing, but now, being ignored, still half dressed, uncomfortably bent over a rail and hair spilling everywhere with her bottom exposed to anyone who was outside, she wasn't as sure.

When she'd first seen him, she'd been intrigued. She'd only been at the party a few minutes when she'd wandered to the window. She'd watched him accept a beer. He'd nodded politely to the pretty submissive who'd fetched it for him.

Some guests, Doms and Dommes alike, ignored servers, but this cowboy seemed to have old-world manners.

She'd intentionally timed her walk across the patio. As she'd exaggeratedly moved her hips, hoping to catch his attention, she'd prayed she wouldn't fall off her ridiculously high heels.

When she'd noticed Gregorio moving towards Master Michael, she'd gritted her teeth. But obviously, he hadn't been deterred, and it had been all she could do not to pump her fist in joy.

Now, she was wondering if her enthusiasm had been misplaced. Perhaps she should have asked Gregorio about Master Michael before agreeing to play. "Can we get on with it, Sir?"

"When I'm ready."

Damn him. Earlier, when he'd slapped her pussy, she'd nearly orgasmed. Then he'd restrained her ankles and stroked the inside of her thighs. She had been certain he'd start the action quickly. But since then he had barely touched her, just enough to intrigue her. And now impatience was curling in her stomach.

She released her grip on the bars to stretch her fingers.

"I'd like you to stay still, please."

"Yes, Sir," she said, not because she meant it, but because it was expected. She understood his rules, and she'd play by them to get some skin-on-skin satisfaction.

Startling her, he grabbed both of her ass cheeks and squeezed unbelievably hard. She yelped.

"Too much?"

God, no. "It was fine, Sir." Once the immediacy of the pain had receded, a warm glow settled in. No one had done that before, and damn, the surprise had aroused her. She tingled, wondering what was next.

"So is there a reason you're not holding on as you're supposed to be?"

"Sorry, Sir." She grabbed the bars again.

"Do you do that often?"

She frowned. "Sir?"

"Allow your mind to wander?"

"I..."

"Are you always living in the future, Sydney, rather than enjoying the moment?"

"I thought you weren't going to psychoanalyse me, Sir."

He laughed. The sound unnerved her, as if he knew she was trying to goad him into action.

At least fifteen more seconds dragged before he lightly smacked her right buttock. There was no heat. She wondered if this was worth it. The night was young, and there were plenty of other Doms here. She could find someone else, get a few orgasms and be home in bed before eleven.

"Relax." He tapped a few times on her left buttock. "Enjoy it."

She took a deep breath.

He continued the light smacks, hardly varying the intensity but sometimes the location.

She exhaled in a frustrated rush.

"Give me what I want, Sydney, and I'll make sure you get what you want."

"And what do you want?"

He didn't respond. From her upside-down position, she saw him take a step back. "Sir?"

"To move at my speed, little sub. I'm watching your reactions, learning your body. You might be impatient, but you are getting aroused."

Since the light breeze felt cool on her exposed parts, she suspected he might be right. But she knew his slowness and his tenderness might be her undoing.

"I know I'm asking you go outside your comfort zone, maybe beyond what you've experienced before. Would you be willing to trust me for a few minutes?"

"How many is a few?" she asked suspiciously.

"Give me five minutes. After that time, if you're not happy, I'll give you an ass blistering you'll never forget."

Her ass tightened at his words. The first part of his sentence had been kind, the second part clipped. The way he used his voice made her react in a visceral way.

"You'd like that, wouldn't you?"

"Yes," she said, proud of the fact.

"And I'll have a little more respect. You're not going to be punished for your lack of good manners... At least not right now. I don't know the extent of your training, and some couples don't follow protocols. But I've corrected you a couple of times already. And you've continued to leave Sir out of your sentences, and you are not addressing me as Master Michael. Perhaps no one's demanded good behaviour from you before, or maybe you're intentionally being a brat, I don't know. But if we continue on from here, you will comply with my requirements. We can talk about anything that makes you uncomfortable. Do you understand?"

In an underwater competition, she'd gone without breathing for almost three minutes, so surely she could get through this negotiation. "Yes, Sir," she said.

He spanked her right buttock *hard*.

She sucked a breath between her teeth. So, so much better.

"Did I get your attention?" he asked as he rubbed the tender spot.

"Yes, Sir," she said. "Thank you."

"That's better." He grabbed her ass cheeks like he had earlier and squeezed again.

She surrendered to the exquisite pain, letting her body go limp.

"Now, Sydney, I'm going to play with you the way I like to play with submissives. I want to ensure you get off, but this is about what I want, too."

"Of course, Sir." Was that the difference between him and other Doms she'd played with? From the beginning, he wanted it to be a mutually rewarding experience, not about either of them in particular. Some guys seemed all about their own kink. Others seemed so intent on being sure she enjoyed it that things felt mechanical, rote.

He held her around the waist and pressed his body against hers, forcing her into the fence. Denim scratched her skin, and his cock angled suggestively between her cheeks. He rocked his hips, and she moved with him in a dance as primitive as the universal heartbeat.

"You're getting hot for me, Sydney."

Her senses were overwhelmed. "Yes, Sir."

"I like that." He moved back a bit to touch her cunt before sliding his fingers over her hot folds, teasing and arousing. He pressed a thumb against her anal whorl. The fact that she couldn't close her legs made escape impossible. She wriggled, trying to coax him into giving her more.

Master Michael stroked her clit, making her rise onto her toes as much as the restraints allowed. "Oh, Master Michael…"

"That's enough," he said, pulling away entirely.

"But—"

With a sharp smack to her pussy, he cut off her protest.

The pain heightened her desire. She was lost in a delirium of want, desperate to come.

"You're a very sexy woman, Sydney." He kept his fingers pressed to the small of her back.

Before she could reply, he spanked her repeatedly, and hard.

This, this was what she needed.

He fondled her pussy.

"I want to come."

"Ask."

"May I?"

"Soon."

"May I, Sir?"

"That will more likely get you what you want."

But instead of bringing her off, he spanked her again, rapidly, leaving no part of her buttocks unscathed.

Her fingers were now in a death-grip around the metal, and she needed to hold on so the world wouldn't spin out of control.

When she was sure she couldn't take any more, he gently squeezed her clit.

She screamed. "I… Please. I want to come."

Again, maddeningly, he denied her.

Sydney rose as high as she could, thrusting her ass towards him, wordlessly asking, seeking, but her efforts only earned her a pinch on her right thigh.

"Not quite yet," he told her.

It had been a long time since she'd been this turned on, and she craved the release she'd find in an orgasm. "I don't want to wait, Sir."

He laughed again softly. "It will be worth it. I promise."

She felt pressure deep inside, creating a persistent demand.

"Ready for more, Sydney?"

"Yes, yes, *yes*."

He slapped her left buttock, then quickly stroked between her legs. The momentary friction drove her mad. Before she could react, he smacked her right cheek then teased her pussy. On and on he went, relentlessly repeating the pattern, not doing any one thing long enough for her to get off.

What he did instead was set every nerve ending on fire.

As the seconds passed, her resistance receded.

"That's it," he said, his modulated, rich voice sounding as if it came from the farthest mountain peak. "Your butt is turning the prettiest shade of pink. Beautiful, beautiful, Sydney."

She no longer held the bars as tightly, and she didn't struggle as hard against the ankle cuffs. She didn't even wriggle her body in order to press her cunt against his hand when he paused there. Instead, she surrendered.

The world seemed to spin backwards, and she stopped being concerned that they were out in the open. She no longer noticed her earlier discomfort. In fact, her body felt as if it were weighed down beneath a thousand stinging sensations.

"Even more?"

"Oh..." She was already delirious.

"We can stop now, and I can give you the orgasm you've earned. Or we can continue with my belt."

Sydney shivered. He'd already taken her past the limits of how long she thought she could hold off her orgasm, and the curious part of her wanted to know what else was possible. "Please," she said. "I want more."

"Please..." he prompted.

"Please, Sir."

"To be clear, Sydney, are you begging?"

"I'm begging," she said. "Just tell me you're taking off your belt, Sir." She was aware of her moisture. And of a small amount of tension in her muscles that she hadn't noticed earlier.

"I'm taking off my belt," he affirmed.

Arousal skipped through her. For the first time, she wondered what he might look like naked. She'd noticed the breadth of him, the long, lean length of his legs and his tight ass. She'd bet he wasn't a ranch owner who let the hired hands do all the work—the calluses on his fingers proved it. "And your hat?"

"That might happen later," he told her.

Later.

When they'd first talked, he'd mentioned going back to his place, but she'd been convinced that wasn't going to happen. She hadn't told him that, but she believed chemistry, as he'd called it, was nothing more than a word to make insatiable romantics swoon.

She had planned to live by her personal motto—show up and hook up. She'd mingle, look for unattached Doms, introduce herself then see if a private room was available.

Now, she wanted to see where the evening might go.

Sydney moaned and writhed when he let the belt fall across her back. She wished now he'd had her strip. She longed to feel its caressing bite on her bare skin.

She tried to stay quiet and still, knowing he wouldn't be rushed.

The impending orgasm loomed more distantly, leaving her edgy.

She was more than ready when he landed the first couple of strokes across her buttocks. Her skin was already warmed from his earlier squeezes and spanks, and these gentle strokes seemed to blaze.

Although he was nowhere near her pussy, arousal returned full force.

"I'd like you to thrust your ass out for me. And keep it there. If things get to be too much, I'll notice by the way you pull away. When and if you want more, offer yourself to me. And you're always free to use your slow word or your safe word."

Before he was done speaking, she'd presented her rear end as much as possible.

He laid several more strokes across her heated skin, turning her inside out.

"I feel as if I'm going to come, Sir," she told him.

"I'd like that."

She tried to squeeze her legs together, needing just a little pressure, but the confounded man had been clever in his restriction.

He increased the intensity of his swings and she cried out, feeling the leather's bite. This was exactly what she'd been seeking.

Despite her best intention of staying in one position, the force of his blows made her sway. But within moments, it was as if they'd found a rhythm that worked for both of them.

"Red is my new favourite colour," he told her. "And now to add some to the backs of your thighs."

She'd been certain it couldn't get any better. But it did.

He used infinitely less pressure on her legs, but the lashing was just as exquisite.

Slammed against the railing by his relentlessness, she loosened her grip and allowed herself to move freely.

She wasn't sure how long he continued—all she knew was that she was no longer thinking about anything but the moment. Being halfway upside down combined with the Den's mountainous elevation caused a mild oxygen deprivation, leaving her unable to speak.

For the first time in a scene, she realised she wasn't trying to set the pace or manipulate her Dom. She'd given him total control.

It took her several moments to register the fact that he'd stopped.

Her heart rate increased. She blinked to try to clear her mind.

"You did well," he said.

He cupped her heated pussy and squeezed.

"Sir..." The word was a moan wrapped in a breathless plea.

"Come," he said.

He scraped her clit with a fingernail and she screamed, jerking, trembling, feeling as if she were flying apart.

But he didn't let her down gently. Instead, he inserted a finger in her moist heat, finger-fucking her while he put pressure on her clit. He kept it up until she was shaking, her hips pistoning. Orgasm after orgasm claimed her. And when she was convinced she had nothing left, he abraded one of the welts on her left buttock.

She arched her back, pushing away from the fencing, allowing him in deeper and unintentionally increasing the force of his touch against her clitoris.

Sydney screamed as she shattered again. She was breathless, overwhelmed, more satisfied than she'd been in months, if not years.

She gasped for breath. Her body was drenched in sweat, and her thoughts were scrambled.

"You're about warmed up," he said.

Warmed up? Her knees sagged. It was a good thing she was bent over, otherwise his softly spoken words would have made it impossible for her to support her own weight.

She was aware of him unfastening her ankles then rubbing her bare legs. Although the touch wasn't erotic, it sent a warm shiver through her.

"Stay where you are," he instructed.

As if she could move.

Master Michael took control, tugging her dress back into place before he effortlessly lifted her from the ground, scooping her into his arms.

She prided herself on her strength, and she'd never been a snuggler. But he'd worn her out and she was powerless to do anything other than wrap one arm around his neck and lay her cheek against his chest. She breathed in his power and strength, and the pine scent of his soap. He felt…comforting.

He snatched up the blanket and strode towards the patio.

"My shoes."

"I'll get them in a minute," he said.

Near the fire pit, he placed her in a chair then wrapped the blanket around her.

"I'll be right with you," he said.

She watched him return to the fence to pick up her shoes and the cuffs. Her strappy heels dangled from his index finger, and she wondered why she found the sight so sexy.

He returned to her and dropped the shoes and cuffs into an untidy pile before signalling for a server.

Master Michael snagged two bottles of water from the man's tray, then uncapped one for her. As he offered it to her, he asked, "How are you feeling?"

"I…" She hesitated. She curled her hands around the bottle. Instead taking a drink, she regarded him over the top. She generally kept her thoughts and emotions to herself. She had a few very close friends, some from college, still, but she chose how much she shared, even with them.

The wood in the fire pit crackled and hissed, and the light cast intriguing shadows over him. Finally, she settled for a non-committal answer. "You were right... You made me beg."

He leaned over her, bracing his hands on the chair arms, and said, "That was only an appetiser, Sydney."

They were so close, they breathed the same air. "Is that a promise?"

He pressed one of his thumbs to her lips. "Take it any way you want to."

She shuddered.

For a moment she wondered if he was going to kiss her. But that seemed too personal. She blinked as he pulled away.

He used a booted foot to drag in another chair then he sat next to her.

She'd got so much more than expected here tonight, and she still had on everything except her underwear that he hadn't given her back...and she'd yet to see him naked. He was right about one thing—what they'd shared had definitely whetted her appetite. Now she wanted the main course.

Although there were many other couples milling about, he'd positioned them so she felt cocooned, as if it were just the two of them on the vast acreage.

She sipped her water and noticed Gregorio and the Den's owner, Master Damien, looking in their direction. Master Damien looked rakish. The cuffs of his long-sleeved white shirt were folded back, exposing his forearms. His hair was longer than it had been the last time she'd seen him, and she wondered how many subs, men and women alike, longed to run their fingers through it. To her knowledge, though, he played with no one. His history was an object of frequent discussion, but the man himself provided no answers.

Gregorio stood next to his boss, shoulder to shoulder. If she wasn't mistaken, Gregorio was smiling.

A woman with incredibly long, dark hair joined him. A much, much larger man, apparently her sub, knelt next to them with his head bowed. Even while she talked with Gregorio, she kept her hand affectionately on top of her sub's head.

The man cocked his head a little, looking up at his Domme. It could be her imagination, but the man looked peaceful in a way she'd never experienced.

"Mistress Catrina," Master Michael said as if reading her thoughts. "She's training a new submissive."

"Training? They're not a couple?"

"No. To my knowledge, Catrina doesn't have permanent submissives."

"And how about you?" she asked. When he didn't answer, she glanced at him. The brim of his damnable hat made his expression unreadable. She wanted to see his eyes.

"No."

The answer was abrupt and didn't invite further questions.

Saying nothing more, he steepled his fingers and looked over the top of his hands at the fire.

"Never?" she prodded.

He glanced her way. "It hasn't worked out that way."

"You've never collared a woman?"

"No."

"You're an expert at one syllable answers, Sir."

"If—when—appropriate, Ms Wallace, I'll have no secrets from you."

"Oh?"

He turned to face her. "And you'll have none from me."

She shivered a little, despite the fire, despite the blanket, despite the leather dress.

"So, little sub, is this goodnight?" he asked. "Or would you like to come home with me?"

Little sub? No one had called her that before. And truthfully, if they had, she might have run, or as forcefully as possible let them know it wasn't acceptable. She liked a bit of adventure with her sex. But submission? That really wasn't her thing. As an occasional part of the act, it was fine. But she wanted nothing more, and if they continued, she'd have to make sure she set him straight about that.

Still… There was something about the way he said those words—tinged with a roughened, raw huskiness—that made them palatable. They sounded like a term of endearment, and that made something forbidden uncurl within her. "What do you have in mind?" If he was offering another ride on this extremely emotional and physical rollercoaster, she was intrigued.

She was sexually satisfied, but the husky tone of his voice and her wild imagination were enough to interest her again. He'd piqued that insatiable need in her, the one that left her restless, always wanting to know what else was out there.

"I haven't seen you naked." He swept his gaze down her body. "I haven't had you on your knees. And I haven't tormented your nipples."

Damn. "I have very sensitive nipples, Sir."

"Do you?" he asked, sounding unconcerned. "Then having me drag you onto your toes by them will no doubt be uncomfortable."

The idea made her shift in her seat.

"So what will it be, Sydney?" he asked again. "Would you like to continue? Or shall we say goodnight?"

She noticed that his cock strained against the denim. Suddenly she felt hungry for him. She wanted him inside her, filling her again and again. She had to have a taste… "I'd like to continue."

He raised his eyebrows. "Then address me correctly."

"*Sir*. I'd like to continue, Sir."

"At the ranch? Or would you be more comfortable here?"

Staying at the Den had numerous advantages. Gregorio and Master Damien would both look out for her. But she was curious about Master Michael and how he lived.

"I'm happy to drive to your place, if that's best for you," he continued.

"In Evergreen?" She shook her head. Not only did it not make sense for him to drive back towards Denver, but she didn't invite men to her condominium. She liked her privacy, and she always wanted the freedom to get in her vehicle and leave when she was ready. "Your place is fine."

He stood and offered his hand. She accepted it. Effortlessly, he tugged her up and held onto her hand far longer than she had expected. A protective part of her brain urged her to pull away. But the far more primitive, feminine receptors recognised his strength, power and masculinity. She couldn't move.

"I'm happy to drive you," he said. "Your vehicle will be fine here, but I assume you'd prefer to take your own car?"

"Yes, Sir."

He nodded. "Just as well. I'd require you to keep your dress lifted, and the sight of your bare cunt would distract me."

The things he said were an erotic thrill.

After releasing her, he folded the blanket and picked up the cuffs while she slid back into her heels. She half expected him to ask or even instruct her to carry them, but he didn't.

His behaviour struck her as odd. It had been her experience that most Doms expected subs to act in specific ways. But other than his request that she call him Sir, he seemed unconcerned about anything else. He was a puzzle.

He nodded to indicate that she should precede him.

"I like watching your hips move and remembering the red marks on your cheeks."

Earlier she'd intentionally tried to capture his interest with her walk, but now that she was aware of his scrutiny, she felt self-conscious.

"Sexy," he said.

Master Damien detached himself from the group he'd been visiting with and met them midway across the patio.

Master Michael placed a hand lightly on her shoulder. Knowing she had no choice, she stopped.

"Thanks for your hospitality," Master Michael said, accepting Master Damien's extended hand.

"Always a pleasure. You're leaving already?"

"We are."

Master Damien raised one of his impossibly dark eyebrows and looked at her directly. "Is everything all right, Sydney?"

This was one thing she had always appreciated about the Den. Damien and Gregorio enforced the rules, and looked after the safety of all their guests. "Yes. Everything is fine, thank you." Master Michael tightened his grip on her shoulder, and she said, "I mean yes, Sir."

"May I have a moment with Sydney?"

"Of course," Master Michael said. "I'll be inside."

She watched until he had entered the house and handed the cuffs and blanket to a perfectly trained sub. The woman extended her hands, keeping her gaze down as she moved off.

"You've never left with anyone," Master Damien observed. "And Master Michael is not your usual type."

She waited for him to say something further, but he didn't. She marvelled at his patience. Master Damien was correct—she usually scened with Doms whose reputation she knew, men who would give her what she wanted without asking for anything more.

The instant attraction to Master Michael when she'd seen him talking with Gregorio had been something more visceral. She liked how tall he was, how broad, how focused and, of course, the fact that he was willing to form his own opinions about her. "He's different," she said finally. "Gentle's not the right word." She met Master Damien's gaze and sighed. "But I can't think of a better one. Measured, maybe. Calculated."

He nodded. "Don't underestimate him."

A small shiver traced her spine. "Are you saying I shouldn't trust him?"

"Not at all."

"Then…"

"I've known Master Michael for eight years, maybe more. He plays by his own rules."

She'd already ascertained that. During their brief encounter near the fence, he'd moved at his speed, not hers, but there was no doubt she'd got what she needed. Maybe more than she'd been anticipating. "Ah, I get it. You're concerned for him, rather than me," she said with a smile.

"Perhaps I am."

"Ouch."

He grinned, taking the sting out of his words. "If you need anything, feel free to telephone us here."

She nodded. "Thank you, Sir."

Master Michael was waiting for her inside the patio doors. He had her purse in hand. Oddly, it didn't detract from his masculinity.

"I had your car brought around."

She accepted the small handbag. "Thank you."

He captured her chin with his thumb and forefinger. "Unless you've changed your mind?"

"You don't scare me," she said, meeting his gaze. His eyes were a deep, dark green, as unreadable as they were inviting.

"Maybe I should," he said.

The pseudo-threat sent a jolt of adrenaline through her. While he kept her gaze and chin imprisoned, he swept a fingertip across her jawbone. "I'll follow you," she said, feigning a calm that had suddenly deserted her. As Master Damien had pointed out, she didn't go home with men, and Master Michael was nothing like other Doms she played with. But his complexity intrigued her. She'd known him only a short time yet she'd already figured out he was as demanding emotionally as he was physically. The physical part excited her. The emotional one...? That she could do without.

"Shall we?" he asked.

She nodded.

He slowly released his hold then placed his fingers against the small of her back and guided her towards the front of the home. An attendant, nattily dressed as if he were a doorman at a New York City hotel—minus a shirt—wished them a good evening.

That he drove a new but dusty, oversized pickup truck didn't surprise her. The jeans, cowboy hat and worn leather boots were obviously not just for effect.

She followed him out of the secluded area where the Den was nestled, and they turned left onto Highway 34, heading north. There were distant peaks, seemingly endless miles of high mountain prairie, but very few headlights from oncoming cars. It was as if they had the world to themselves.

Rather than getting nervous, the kind of anticipation that came from the unknown raced through her. She cranked up the stereo, blasting dance music throughout the passenger compartment of her decade-old small sports utility vehicle.

She kept his tail lights in sight, and she appreciated that he drove a bit over the speed limit. About half an hour later, they left the tarmac behind. A large pothole in a bumpy dirt road almost jarred the wheel from her hands.

This definitely hadn't been what she'd planned when she had shimmied into the leather dress several hours ago. In fact, out here, the dress and shoes seemed ridiculous.

They bypassed a number of turn-offs and she had to drop back in order to not get blasted by the dirt spewing behind his tyres.

A few minutes later, he followed a fork to the right. She was starting to wonder if it was a road to nowhere when he braked to a stop in front of a fence. It was buttressed by massive, rough-hewn wooden poles that soared at least twenty feet in the air. A beam spanned the overhead distance, and a metal sign hung from chains. A large raptor with talons extended was emblazoned on the left side, next to the words *Eagle's Bend Ranch.*

With his hat still firmly in place, the lord and master of the place unlocked the gate before walking back to her vehicle. She rolled down the window.

"Welcome," he said. "Follow me through the gate. I'll close it behind us." He placed his hands on the door and leaned in.

Damn, he smelt good—of rugged, open space.

"Scared yet?"

"Not a chance."

He grinned then. "That's my girl."

The easy familiarity took her by surprise. No one had called her anything like that. Nasty sex words, yes. Syrupy, sugary, hoping-to-get-you-to-bed words like honey and baby, yes. But something that innocuous? Definitely not. It didn't fit her. So why the hell was she smiling back at him?

Without another word, he turned away. She watched as he climbed back into the truck then drove through, stopping a fair distance away.

She pulled in behind him, then watched in the rear-view mirror as he strode back to secure the chain and lock again.

Now she was nervous. He'd effectively blocked her escape.

He stopped by her vehicle again.

"The code for the lock is M-Y-H-M," he said. "Shorthand for my home, so it's easy to remember."

She exhaled. "How did you know?"

"Honey, you haven't blinked in thirty seconds. Not much scares you, does it?"

Sydney slowly shook her head.

"But the things that scare you are debilitating."

"There you go with the psychoanalysis again."

"Nah. That's just casual observation. I'll let you know what I see when I really have the chance to study you."

Before she could respond, he'd moved off. She rolled up her window and followed him towards a house. Off to the right were a number of buildings, a barn among them.

More lights came on as they drove, obviously all equipped with motion sensors. He indicated a place for her to park near a large pine tree.

He was there to help her from the vehicle, something she appreciated with her heels and the uneven dirt parking area. "This outfit isn't exactly the best for ranch wear," she said, closing the car door.

"Are you kidding? It's perfect."

In the distance, she heard an occasional moo that she assumed came from a cow and something that sounded like the bleating of a goat. While she also lived in the mountains, it was as if she and Master Michael occupied two entirely different universes.

He cupped her elbow and drew her towards the house. A huge yard was also fenced, but with horizontally notched wooden poles interlaced with vertical ones. Though it was likely practical, it was also artistic.

With one hand still on her, he opened the gate, taking time to ensure it latched securely behind them.

"To keep Chewie out," he said.

"Chewie?"

"Long story. She's a Nigerian dwarf goat."

"I thought ranches had cows."

"I run cattle, yes," he said. "But Chewie is more of a pet. Well, maybe a pest. She would eat all the grass and the flowers and the trees if I let her near the house. Well, and anything else she could find."

"And the fence stops her?"

"It's supposed to. I'm thinking of putting up a surveillance camera. Somehow the gate gets opened far too often. Last I checked, she had hooves rather than opposable thumbs, but I wonder..."

The sight of columbines and other wildflowers surprised her. "Are you the gardener?"

"No. That's thanks to my sister. She doesn't visit often, but she plants, I don't know...stuff. Annuals. Perennials. Bulbs. Seeds. Bushes. Shrubs. As if I'm supposed to know the difference? The goat is hers, and she has a horse here, too. The ranch has a couple of hands. They stay in the bunkhouse over there. Don't worry. We'll have our privacy. And it won't matter how long or how hard you scream—no one will come running to save you."

She looked up. He wasn't smiling, and there'd been no hint of a tease in his tone. A thrill shot through her. It was as if he knew how to turn her on with only a few carefully placed words.

He opened the front door and ushered her inside.

The home was rustic, with exposed-beam ceilings, hardwood floors, hand-woven rugs and oversized leather furniture. A stone fireplace dominated the living room, and wood crisscrossed in the grate, waiting to be lit. Dozens of photographs, some in black and white, crowded the mantel.

Just that detail highlighted the differences in their priorities. She had a single picture of her parents. In the small framed picture, she was about a year old and asleep in the pack on her dad's back. They'd been trekking Nepal at the time, if she remembered the story right.

Her condominium lacked the homey touches that his home had. Hers was impersonal enough to be a hotel room. Until now, that had never bothered her.

"Can I get you something to drink?"

She followed him into the kitchen, aware of the staccato sound of her shoes on the rustic floors. "Water is fine, thank you," she said as she placed her purse on the counter.

He poured her a glass from a pitcher stored in the stainless steel refrigerator.

She accepted it with a smile of thanks and slid onto a bar stool tucked beneath a poured concrete island. The kitchen looked like a designer's dream, with gleaming pots hanging overhead. She rarely cooked, but she appreciated the gas range, the two ovens and miles of countertops.

"I think, Sydney, we should get a few things straight between us." He moved in closer, standing on the other side of the island.

With her hands wrapped around the glass, she looked at him. He folded his arms across his chest. The brim of his hat, as always, cast him in shadows, making it difficult to read his expression.

"Your feedback, verbally as well as physically, matters to me, so I insist on open and honest communication. I want you to get off, and that's more likely to happen if you're interacting with me. I have no interest in just spanking you until you come."

That sounded all right with her. She took a sip of water and squirmed in her seat. Because he demanded a response, she said, "I agree, Sir."

"When I request something from you, I anticipate you will either let me know it's problematic or you'll do as you're told." He raised an eyebrow.

His firm tone brooked no refusal. She took another drink of water to soothe her suddenly dry throat. After releasing the glass, she said, "Yes, Sir."

"In that case, strip and kneel. Hands behind your neck, head tipped back, chest thrust towards me. I promised you I'd torture your nipples."

Chapter Three

Maybe he should have heeded Gregorio's warning.

Michael didn't consider himself much of a risk-taker. He weighed his decisions carefully and he liked having everything in order. Keeping the family's ranch after his parents had passed had never been a question. Although his sister had voted in favour of selling, he hadn't been swayed. His roots went deep into the land. The acreage was as important to him as his next breath.

Yet he couldn't help his attraction to Sydney's untamed streak.

Since his divorce, he'd been careful to play only with women he had met at the Den, and most times he scened with subs who wore the house's purple wrist band and therefore had no expectations of a continuing relationship. They were professionals who knew all the protocols and expectations and could be counted on to behave perfectly.

Sydney, on the other hand, seemed focused on herself. It was all about her, not him, and definitely not about submission.

But he was honest enough to admit that he'd loved the way she'd behaved when he'd had her draped over the fence. Her responses had been real with no artifice. When he'd brought her to orgasm for the first time, he'd known he'd rather spend the evening with her than anyone else, no matter how well trained they were.

He shouldn't see her as a challenge, but he did.

Slowly, she slid from the bar stool.

The dress hugged her curves, showing off her body. She looked so sexy it was almost a shame to have her remove the garment. Almost.

Michael stayed where he was while she pulled up the leather, revealing her skin a beautiful inch at a time.

He'd seen her naked from the waist down, so he knew her pussy had no hair. Her legs were shapely and, if luck held, her buttocks might still be pink from his belt.

But as she shimmied about, pulling the dress over her head, he took in the whole of her. She had an athletic build, not overly thin, and she had definite curves, along with a waist made for his hands. Her breasts were perfect, not too big, with nipples that were already hard.

She laid the dress over the stool then bent to remove her shoes.

"Leave them on," he said.

"Of course, Sir."

For a moment, she stood there and he simply looked at her. Right now, this evening, she was his.

Without being instructed again, she lowered herself to the floor and placed her hands behind her back as he'd requested.

Her chest rose and fell quickly, and he appreciated the betrayal of nerves. She projected an aura of confidence that appealed to him, but that he had some effect on her made him needy. His cock swelled, but he'd had a hard-on for the better part of two hours. He could wait a little longer.

He walked around her, knowing she was aware of the sound of his boots against the wood. To her credit, she didn't turn to look at him. "Good," he said. "That will help you earn an orgasm."

"Earn, Sir?"

"Please me," he reminded her, "and I'll make sure you are sated."

"That's a tall order, Sir. I'm not sure I've ever been that satisfied."

"Is that another challenge, little sub?"

"No, Sir. That would be wrong. I'm just making a comment."

He grinned. *Yeah.* He would have been smart to have heeded Gregorio's warning. "Cup your breasts, Sydney, and offer them to me."

She did as instructed, drawing them together and lifting them. He crouched in front of her. "Look at me," he told her.

Their gazes met.

Earlier, he'd noticed that her eyes were ice-blue. But he'd seen her outside—the sun had been fading, and the flickering firelight and torches had hidden the richness of the colour. He wondered if she had any idea how expressive their depths were. Now he saw anticipation there, along with a hint of trepidation. "You said your nipples are sensitive."

"Yes, Sir. They are."

He brushed the pads of his thumbs across the tips. She trembled. *Yeah.* If *that* gentle a touch caused that reaction, then nipple play would bring them both endless delights. "I want you to stay as you are, even if you're tempted to move. Understand?"

She nodded.

"And your slow word?"

"*Tur-tle*," she said, breaking the word into two distinct syllables. "Sir," she added.

"That will get you an orgasm denial."

"Not a punishment?" She scowled.

"That is punishment for you. I think you'd like another spanking, and you'll get one. But I'm betting that keeping you on the edge and making you practise patience would really be torment."

She opened her mouth as if to say something, but then closed it again.

"Wise choice," he approved. Still looking at her, he dragged his thumbnails across the tips of her nipples.

She sucked in a little breath.

He pinched her nipples lightly then let go right away. Even though she swayed towards him a little, she kept her eyes open, her gaze focused on his face. "Good girl," he said.

This time, he took her nipples and used more pressure, squeezing for longer.

"Ahh..."

"They're like little pebbles," he said.

"Yes, Sir. It...hurts."

"Do you want to stop?"

"No."

He released her, giving her a short break, letting her process the sensations, making her wonder what was next.

"Keep holding your breasts for me." After she nodded, he repeated the process twice. She closed her eyes before quickly opening them. "Ready for more?"

"Yes, Sir."

He increased the tempo, pinching her harder, longer. He'd been giving her a handful of seconds to recover and prepare for the next assault—he now shortened the time between the breaks. All the while, he held her gaze, watching her eyes for signs of real distress. "Is your pussy getting wet?"

"I'm not sure, Sir."

"You're not sure?"

"I'm a bit overwhelmed."

"Check."

"Sir?"

"With your right hand. Feel your pussy."

She blinked, as if confused for a moment, but she let go of her breast and moved her hand between her legs.

"Well?" he asked.

"Yes, I'm a bit wet, Sir."

"Show me your hand."

Unbelievably, her face was turning pink. Was she embarrassed? She came across as confident and secure, almost flippant in her attitude. Especially after Gregorio's warning, seeing this side of her surprised him. Could it be that no one else had taken the time to proceed cautiously with her, to demand her participation?

She held up her hand and he saw moisture on her fingertips.

"That's perfect," he said. He captured her wrist and lowered his head to taste her juices. "Delicious. Musky. I like how sensitive your nipples are and how you respond to my touch," he said. "It pleases me immensely. Please, continue to play with your pussy. Use both hands."

"Yes, Sir." She lowered her head and dropped her gaze to the floor.

"No, no. I want you to keep looking at me."

After blinking, she refocused on him.

"Better," he said. "Much, much better. I always want to see your expression. I want to make sure you're enjoying yourself." That was especially important if he couldn't always trust that she'd use her safety words. "And I want to make sure you don't come."

"But—"

"Do it *now*."

She slowly moved both hands between her legs.

"That's it. Spread your labia with your left hand. Use your right to slide across your clit and to finger-fuck yourself." As he gave his instructions, he tugged on her nipples.

"Oh, Sir…"

"Do you like that?"

"It's… Sir… Yes. I do." She moved her hips and did as he said.

Damn, she was hot. "Beautiful," he approved. "Pleasure yourself. Enjoy. Surrender." He tormented her nipples and kept a close eye on her reactions, determined to give her what she needed without hurting her too much. "That's a good little sub."

"Yes, Sir," she whispered.

He noticed that the deeper she slid into their scene, the easier it seemed for her to call him Sir.

At the Den, even when he'd moved her towards the fence, her back had been straight. It was as if she affected a certain posture to keep others at a distance. But here, now, with his attention solely on her, with no one else around, her shoulders were more relaxed.

As he continued to rapidly pinch, pull and release, she added a second finger to her cunt.

He smelt her arousal. His cock rose in insistent response. He wanted to claim her, mark her as his. "Ride it," he encouraged.

She was getting closer and closer. Her breaths were rapid, and her moans became more pronounced.

Her head fell back and she gave a little cry, a warning he recognised. "*Stop!*"

Ignoring him, she continued to work her hand against her pussy.

He moved quickly, releasing his grip on her breasts to grab her hands.

"What?" she demanded.

He pulled her hands above her head and secured both of her wrists with one of his hands.

She exhaled a shaky breath. "I... Damn you. I almost came," she said. Her nostrils were flared, her mouth slightly parted and her hair was in disarray.

"And I told you orgasm denial was part of your punishment. You haven't earned an orgasm." He leaned in a bit. "The fact you just forgot your manners can be overlooked for now, but if you have any hope of being allowed to come, you need to focus on me."

She drew her eyebrows together and pursed her lips.

He wondered if she was going to tell him to go to hell and use her safe word, grab her keys and head for the door.

He watched, fascinated, as her internal emotional battle played out on her face. She clenched her teeth and set her chin. He said nothing, giving her time to process what was happening. He knew they were on a precipice, and damn, he wished he knew the right way to pull them back.

She was definitely headstrong and unaccustomed to giving up control. From the beginning, he'd known she liked BDSM for the intensity, but he'd bet she hadn't reckoned on this.

Over the course of thirty seconds, she remained rigid, glaring at him. Then she took a couple of deep, shuddering breaths and the tension seemed to drain from her body.

He released a breath he hadn't realised he'd been holding. "No doubt I'm different from anyone you've played with," he said quietly. And she was unlike anyone he'd ever known. His wife hadn't been this complex. She'd enjoyed their sexual interactions, at least up until he'd put a ring on her finger.

Sydney tried to extricate her hands, but since she hadn't used her safe word, he kept hold of her. "No doubt I demand things from you that you're not expecting."

"I..."

He waited.

"You're right. I'm used to having an intense physical session."

He nodded.

"I've been with Doms who practised orgasm denial before, but not like this."

"Tell me what you mean."

"They've always just changed tactics so I didn't come as fast. But then, when I did, it was an amazing experience. I've never had it as punishment." She blinked. "I'm not sure I like it."

"Fair enough. You're not meant to. I figured you would happily take a red ass or a flogging on your back. You could feel good that you were being punished for your bad behaviour, but you would really just be getting what you wanted." He traced a finger over one of her eyebrows. Her nipples were still hard, but he noticed she had some goosebumps on her flesh. She'd obviously sweated a little, and now her skin was cooling. Or maybe he'd just unnerved her. "I need you to know one thing—I won't be goaded. And you can stop any time."

"I don't admit defeat."

"That's what I want you to accept." Michael shook his head. "It's about being honest."

"In that case, I wanted to come."

"I can have you back there again in minutes."

"You may not be done punishing me," she said, "but I'm so over being punished. Can we move onto something more fun?"

"I'm afraid you don't get to decide that."

She sighed. "It was worth a try."

"Tell me what you think your orgasm will be like?"

"Will it happen in this century?" she countered. "I mean, will it happen this century, *Sir*?"

He chuckled and released her wrists. "Put your hands behind your back. Spread your knees farther apart."

She scowled and did as requested.

"You wanted me to take off my hat," he said. He removed it and flicked his wrist to send the hat onto the wooden table top, dragging his other hand through his short hair.

"It's lighter than I expected, Sir. I want to get my fingers in it."

"You can hold it when you're on top of me."

"Promise, Sir?"

She definitely should have come with a warning label.

He lay on the floor and shifted so that his face was beneath her. "Your clit is still swollen." He took hold of her waist and pulled her down, forcing her legs farther apart and bringing her lower so that her pussy was mere inches from his face. "Keep your hands where they are. Now move your hips."

"Dear God."

He grasped her labia and tugged. "This skin was made for clamps."

She jerked at the words.

"That's a girl. Keep moving. Just like that."

"This is embarrassing, Sir."

"Get your clit on my tongue or it will be a cold day in hell before you have that orgasm."

She moved, and he took the opportunity to pinch her clit. Yelping, she jerked, and the movement threw her off balance, bringing her cunt into contact with his mouth. Exactly what he'd hoped would happen.

He licked her from back to front.

"I..."

"Fuck my face, little sub."

The position was obviously awkward for her, but she did so. He tongued her, sucked her clit, captured her around the legs and held her prisoner. He ate her, showing his appreciation as she moaned and writhed helplessly. He brought her to the edge then stopped.

"Damnable man, Sir."

He grinned and went back to work. This time, he stuck his tongue in her, savouring the feminine taste.

She rose up onto her knees, off his face, even though he tried to hold her in place.

"That's... It's too much, Sir."

"Not nearly enough," he countered. "Please get back into place."

Her muscles were tight as she complied.

He used his tongue to make her wet and to lap up her juices. He adored her taste. She made soft mewling sounds, and her body stiffened. He immediately stopped what he was doing.

"Argh!"

"Nice try. But your body gave you away. You'll not be sneaking in any orgasms, I'm afraid." He let her go and smacked her right ass cheek. "Kneel up properly." When she did, he moved out from beneath her.

He rose to stand in front of her. She tilted her head back to look at him. Her lips were parted and her eyes were wide. The earlier hostility was gone. Her hands were still linked behind her back as he'd requested. Despite her apparent frustration, she seemed softer somehow. "In answer to your question, no. It appears your orgasm will not be happening this century."

"Master Michael, you are a beast."

"Indeed," he agreed. "I'm open to you convincing me otherwise."

"How, Sir?"

"That's a good start." He reached down to grasp her nipples again. Since he believed in keeping his promises, he said, "Stand."

He pulled on the tips, lengthening her nipples and stretching her breasts.

She grabbed his arms for support and hissed through clenched teeth. He continued until she was standing. "Let go of me," he instructed. "Surrender."

Eyes wide with total trust, she did.

He kept up the pressure until she was on her toes. "Beautiful," he told her. "How does it feel?"

"Oh, damn, Sir... It hurts."

"Was it too much?"

"Yes. And not enough."

He understood, and he delighted in her. Abruptly he released her, only to gather her in his arms and pull her close. She snuggled against him, her chest heaving. He smoothed her hair then cradled her head. He placed his other hand on her back. "You're a brave little sub." After she pulled back, he said, "You've almost earned that orgasm."

She looked up. "Sir?"

"My bedroom is upstairs. I'd like you to crawl up the stairs." He knew what he was asking from her. She liked the intensity of a spanking and, he'd bet, a beating. She wanted to lose herself, let go, push the outer edges of a pain-induced adrenaline rush. But this... He was asking her to do something because it turned him on. "Your choice," he reminded her. "But I want to watch your ass move."

"I'm beginning to think that's one of your kinks."

"It wasn't. Until I saw you walk across the patio at the Den. Now all I can think of is your ass. And I'm wondering if it's red enough."

"I created a monster, Sir."

"You did. So is it? Your ass? Is it red enough?"

"Why do you ask? Didn't you spank it, Sir?"

No doubt she'd earned her reputation at the Den. "Up the stairs. If it's easier, I can fetch a leash."

Her wide-eyed innocent look vanished as she blinked several times in rapid succession. "I can manage on my own, Sir."

She pulled away from him, and he reluctantly let her go.

With athletic grace, she lowered herself to all fours.

"Wait a moment," he said. "We'll go upstairs soon."

She remained in position but looked at him with a frown.

He crossed to a kitchen drawer filled with all sorts of random items and dug through it until he found two small clips. They weren't as serviceable as proper nipple clamps, but since his toys were upstairs, these would work for now. He tested their grip on his pinkie to be sure she wouldn't find them unbearable. Satisfied, he returned to her.

Her breasts hung freely, and he'd never seen anything more enticing. "Since your nipples are already sore, these will intensify the sensation." He bent to fondle her left breast, smacking it back and forth until she gasped. Then he brutally squeezed it. "I haven't even touched your nipple and already it's getting harder."

"Yes, Sir."

"Do you want me to clamp it?"

She turned her head to look at him. "Do it. Please."

"My pleasure." He twisted her nipple then released the clip onto it, not right at the edge as that would cause her too much pain, but a little farther back so that she could tolerate the tension.

He tugged on the makeshift clamp, making sure it was secure. "It should stay on," he said. "It would probably hurt if it came off accidentally." He flicked it a couple of times, just because he could.

She arched her back in unspoken response, but she didn't complain.

"That's a good sub." He thought he heard her growl, but he couldn't be certain. "Shall I place the other or leave you lopsided?"

"I don't suppose we could remove this one so that they'd match, Sir?"

"After all the trouble I've gone to?"

"Of course not. What was I thinking, Sir?"

He moved around her, glad she couldn't see his smile. She looked stunning with that slight arch to her back. Her long blonde hair was in wild disarray, and he was tempted to grab a fistful as he slammed into her from behind.

It took all his self-control to think only about her, about increasing the pleasure of her upcoming orgasm. He could wait. Surely.

He leant down to play with her right breast, plumping it, releasing it. She moaned and moved away from him, so he toyed with the clamp he'd already placed.

"Sir!"

"Sub?"

That she didn't turn and slay him with a look told him she was sinking into the scene. Damn, he liked this, giving her what she wanted, even if she didn't realise that yet. He was certain that when she'd attended this evening's solstice party at the Den, she'd been planning to get a spanking from some random man before saying goodnight and waltzing out of the door. But he hoped this was better, hoped that nothing else could match the high of being with a Dom who was intent on giving her a unique, consuming experience.

He gently swatted her right breast and teased the nipple into an erect state. She dropped her head, and he took advantage of her distraction to place the clamp.

"Oww."

"You'll be all right." He caressed her flesh. "Your swollen nipples look hot." He captured her chin and turned her head so that he could read her expression. Her eyes were wide and they had a glazed look to them, making the blue even more startling. "How's your pussy? Are you getting as turned on as I am?"

"I…" She licked her lower lip.

He felt as if she'd taken a sledgehammer to his solar plexus. The things he could imagine that pink tongue doing…

"Why don't you see for yourself?" she said, the husk in her voice an invitation.

He needed to be careful. She was as smart as she was sassy, and she was adept at manipulation. "I think I will," he said. "Present your ass to me."

"Sir?"

"Move around and put your breasts on the floor."

"That's…"

"Not what you were expecting? Do it."

She moved slowly, as if hoping to minimise the sway of her breasts. Every motion, he knew, would bring a wave of pain to her nipples. But all that would be nothing compared with the agony she'd feel when her breasts were crushed against the wood.

Once she was where he wanted her, he said, "Reach back and spread your buttocks."

He waited while she did as she was told. She readjusted herself several times, obviously to find a more comfortable position. Before she was situated, he toyed with her pussy. "You're definitely wet," he told her as he slid his hand back and forth. "I'd like your permission to put a finger inside you."

"Yes." The word was almost a hiss. "Yes, Sir."

He entered her slowly, and manoeuvred until he felt the difference in the texture of her internal flesh and touched her G-spot.

"Oh! *My God*." She bucked and forced herself back, seeking more.

He indulged her for a few seconds, placing the pad of one thumb lightly against her anal whorl and feathering the lightest of touches over her clit.

"So close," she whispered. "Please, please, please. I want to come. Sir!"

"Not yet." He continued the gentle torture, his cock getting harder and harder. She was so much more responsive than he'd imagined she might be, and seeing her arousal made him horny.

Her words sounded nonsensical, a combination of pleading and demand, all wrapped together.

When he was sure she couldn't take any more without orgasming, he pulled his hands away. "That's a taste of what's to come."

She whimpered, her forehead pressed to the wood, her hands still on her buttocks. He stood and moved to the sink to rinse his hands while she regained her composure.

"Master Michael..."

At the sound of confusion in her tone, he turned off the tap and looked over at her. "Sydney?"

When she didn't respond, he returned to her, devouring the distance in a few brisk strides. "I'm right here." He sat on the floor and gathered her into his arms. Who would have suspected that the toughness she projected was mostly an aura? And he guessed she'd blacken his eye if he even hinted as much to her. She was such an intriguing dichotomy. "Talk to me," he said. "Do you need me to remove the clamps?"

"No." She pushed against his restraint. "There's nothing wrong. I promise."

"Did it bother you that I left you?" He brushed hair back from her face. "Do you hurt?"

"Everything is okay." She sighed, sounding exasperated. "The whole orgasm denial is just driving me crazy. Everything tingles, and there's a gnawing inside me. I haven't felt this way before. Please, don't overreact. I didn't mean to alarm you."

He frowned at her. At best, that was a half-truth. But he suspected he'd get nothing more from her. Still, he liked having her in his arms, inhaling the citrusy scent of her shampoo and touching her bare skin.

"You worry too much, Sir. I'm okay. I always was. I promise."

"I never doubted that," he assured her.

"Can we continue, Sir?"

He debated what to do. Part of him wanted to talk, but maybe she was right. Maybe he'd heard something in her voice that really hadn't been there. A bigger part of him wanted to put each of them out of their misery.

"I am so ready for an orgasm."

"Little sub, you're going to get more than one."

She smiled. "The night is not getting any younger, Sir. And neither am I."

Her momentary weakness was gone, if it had ever really been there. In its place was bravado, but he couldn't help but wonder if it was a façade. Either way, he was more determined than ever to care for her, to give her a different experience than any other Dom ever had.

He loosened his grip. "When you're ready, crawl to the stairs."

She started to move, but then stopped and resumed at a much slower pace.

The trek up the stairs couldn't have been easy. The steps had no carpet, and since the house was old, the pitch was steep. The view, though, was sexually gratifying. If he had his way, he'd keep her here, naked and needy. "Second door on the left," he said. "Kneel up," he instructed when they entered the room. He assumed she'd been around the lifestyle long enough to know what he meant, and clearly she did. She knelt with her legs slightly parted and her hands on her thighs.

He removed all the pillows from the top of the bed and piled them beneath a window. He left the blinds open so the smattering of stars were visible in the inky distance. Since his room was at the back of the house, no one would be able to see in, not that she would mind at any rate.

After pulling back the comforter, he said, "Please get on the bed and lie on your back." As she climbed onto the massive four-poster bed that his father had constructed from local trees, their gazes met. He wasn't a mind reader, but he was convinced he saw trust in the way her eyes were open so wide. If there was anything headier, he had no idea what it was. "I'm going to remove these clamps," he said.

"They're fine, Sir."

"I should have said replace them. I want clovers that will stay on, even if I pull on them."

"Ah… These are fine, Sir. In fact, I've grown quite fond of them."

"As I've mentioned, that's not a decision you get to make." He lowered himself onto the bed next to her and gently plumped her right breast. "This may hurt, but I'll try to mitigate it."

She nodded.

He continued to hold the flesh as he released the clamp. Immediately he replaced the plastic with his mouth. He laved her mistreated flesh with his tongue, helping to stimulate her as the blood flow resumed. She'd arched, but she settled against the sheets again.

"That wasn't as bad as I expected, Sir," she said. "Thank you."

He slowly released his hold on her breast. "I do like it when you're respectful."

She stuck out her tongue then offered a quick explanation, "My lips are dry, Sir."

"Maybe I won't let you come at all."

"Ah…"

"And maybe I'll ejaculate all over your breasts while you watch. Then I'll fall asleep."

"You really do have a sadistic streak, Sir."

"Little sub, you haven't even begun to suspect the depths of my desire to torment you."

She shuddered.

"But you'll find out."

"Should I be scared, Sir?"

"Very." He captured her right hand and moved it to the apex of her thighs. Without warning, he removed the second clamp. He used his mouth to soothe her there, too.

"If that's the treatment I get after you clamp me, feel free to do it anytime."

"My pleasure." And it was. He loved the feminine taste of her and the way her nipple lengthened as he sucked. He used his tongue to press it against the roof of his mouth then gently bit her as he released it.

"Wow, Sir."

"I may play with your breasts for hours."

"At this point, I wouldn't say no."

"I'm going to clamp you again," he said. He raised an eyebrow, waiting for a response.

"Yes, Sir."

"Such an obedient little sub."

She opened her mouth, but he placed a finger across her lips to silence what he knew would be her objection. After she nodded, he removed his finger. "Don't move," he instructed.

He stood and crossed to the leather-covered storage bench at the foot of the bed. He removed a box that had been buried under a comforter. Careful to stay in her sight, he placed the box on a nightstand. He pulled out several pairs of clamps, some scarves, a small bottle of lube and a couple of lengths of sturdy rope.

"Do you have condoms there?" she asked. "Otherwise, my purse is downstairs."

He looked at her. With her eyes wide, mouth softly parted, naked body and reddened breasts, she was beautiful. "You want to fuck?" he asked, his chest constricting. There was nothing he wanted more.

"I want you in me, Sir. Yes."

Suddenly he had difficulty remembering what he was doing. The idea of burying himself balls deep in her pussy scrambled his brains.

He forced himself to think about her. His needs could and would wait. He'd promised her several orgasms, and that was his priority.

She kept her gaze fixed on him as he selected a pair of Japanese clover clamps. For a moment, he allowed the chain to dangle from his index finger.

"Yes," she said.

His cock grew incredibly harder.

He returned to her and sucked on each of her nipples before attaching the rubber-tipped metal clamps.

She lifted her butt off the bed. "It burns, Sir."

"Use your safe word or slow word, or settle down." He stroked between her legs, making her wet again. Within moments, she responded to his touch. He delighted in learning all her nuances.

"Ah..."

He took the chain in hand and gave a gentle tug.

"Damn!"

He slid a finger inside her. "Damn is right, little sub. I think you're turned on." He released the chain before removing his finger. "Turn over and put your forehead on the mattress. Extend your hands so they reach the headboard."

Although she moved slowly, he didn't hurry her.

He wrapped scarves around her wrists to protect her skin then tied them both together. He kept a careful eye on her and listened intently to the sound of her breathing. Her muscles were relaxed, and she inhaled softly. No doubt Sydney liked bondage, something he'd be sure to remember.

After securing the length of sturdy rope to the lowest beam of the headboard, he stepped back to survey his handiwork. "Fabulous." What could be more perfect than a beautiful woman tied in place for him? "How are you doing? Not too uncomfortable?"

She tugged on the bonds, as if testing them. As he'd suspected, they held her in place.

"I'm fine, Sir."

He pulled his shirt from his waistband and began to unfasten the buttons, from the bottom up. She turned her head to the side to watch. He shrugged out of the material and tossed it in the direction of the closet.

"Sexy, if you don't mind me saying so, Sir. And nice tattoo."

"Thank you." It was a good thing the artist had had talent. He'd had too much to drink the night his father had died and, in honour of the man's memory and his own commitment to the land, he'd had an eagle tattooed on his right biceps. "Now to see to you, Sydney."

He stroked her ass. "You're not even a bit pink from your earlier spanking."

She wiggled her hips as if in invitation.

He rubbed her, gradually increasing the friction. Then he smacked her, hard.

"Uhm," she said. The word was all but a sigh.

He spanked the other cheek as well. She seemed to relax even more. Her spine became more supple, and she pressed her cheek onto the mattress.

After giving her more, he used his right hand to unbuckle his belt while he stroked her with the other.

She moved back and forth, wordlessly seeking more from him.

"Do you want to come?"

"Yes. Yes, Sir, I do. *Please.*"

Her plea was almost his undoing. But he wanted her to wait just a little longer. He stopped touching her and finished extracting his belt from its loops. He doubled it over and asked, "How about a taste of leather?"

"More than a taste would be nice."

He gave her a few gentle slaps, searching for a rhythm they'd both enjoy. He'd learnt a bit about her when he'd bent her over the fence at the Den. She could tolerate hard hits—in fact, she seemed to enjoy them the most. It would take a minute to get her there, though, and he forced himself to be patient with how intensely he delivered the blows. While he wanted her red and sore, he also wanted her to recover quickly. He had other plans for her.

With every third hit, he applied a little more wrist. And he rained the leather kisses over her buttocks and the backs of her thighs. Her tiny whimpers drove him on.

"God, Sir, I need to come."

That she became so aroused by an erotic beating appealed to him. He couldn't wait to use a flogger and a paddle on her.

He paused for a moment to tease her pussy.

"Now, now, now," she chanted.

"Almost." He stepped back and resumed the beating until her ass was red.

"I'm going to come without you touching me." Her fingers were interlaced and she strained against the rope binding.

Where she'd been soft, she was now tense. He'd never kept a woman waiting for so long, and never had a sub been more deserving.

Michael threw aside the belt and buried his head between her legs, using his tongue on her pussy, sliding three fingers inside her then back out.

"Sir!"

He didn't respond. He kept licking, lapping her juices, driving her wild. He reached up with one hand and gave the chain that ran between her breasts a vicious yank.

She screamed.

She humped his face and he kept at her, driving her orgasm, not ceasing until she was twitching wildly and sobbing into the sheets.

When she went limp, he stroked her spine with his fingertips. "Now, little sub, I'm going to fuck you thoroughly."

Chapter Four

Shattered.

Sydney was completely, totally shattered.

Despite the bondage, she collapsed, turning on her side. She dragged in several breaths. Even though she'd played with a number of Doms and had had a serious D/s relationship, she'd never experienced anything like this.

"Are you all right?"

"Fine," she mumbled. She blinked, trying to regain her bearings, aware of him moving around the room.

Master Michael had kept her on the edge for at least an hour, and before he'd allowed her a release, he had demanded that she gave everything she'd had to offer. In fact, she was sure he'd asked for more than she'd even known possible. It seemed he wasn't satisfied with her just offering her body unconditionally to him. He wanted more.

The emotional aspects that he'd tapped into tonight bothered her. She'd never felt vulnerable before. She'd always been in control of herself—she set the ground rules with her Dominants and greeted each situation with abandon, riding each powerful experience to a thrilling orgasm. The high she got from each scene kept her sane.

Master Michael, with his gentle yet uncompromising ways, went beyond simple whip-wielding. He'd succeeded in forcing her into a submissive mindset, something she'd always resisted.

"I'll be right with you," he said, his voice rich and husky.

Sydney thought she had nodded, but she couldn't be sure.

She heard water running in the attached bathroom then there was silence. She was grateful for a few moments alone. Unlike earlier, she needed to compose herself before facing him, and oddly, it was his earlier response that had given her the trust to stay on his bed, still bound, waiting. Most times, after she'd been satisfied, she'd thanked the man—taken care of him with a requisite blow job if he had seemed put out—then headed home and back to her life. But this time she was content to stay, at least for a while.

And honestly, now that she'd seen Master Michael's naked chest and the tattoo that matched the brand she'd seen on the sign above the ranch's entrance, she wanted him naked. Getting him off didn't seem as if it would be a chore. In fact, she wanted his cock inside her.

His restraint amazed her. She'd noticed his erection, but he'd kept his attention solely on her. No doubt he had mad bedroom skills. More, though, he'd backed up his arrogant statements. The orgasm *had* been worth waiting for. It had lain curled inside, a throbbing, incessant demand that his strokes and ministrations fed, and when he had shoved her over the edge, it had been as if the physical sensation had clawed its way out.

She wasn't sure how much time had passed when she felt him sit on the mattress behind her. He was a big man, and the mattress was forced to yield to him, just as she had been.

"You'll feel a little dampness," he said.

He ran a cool washcloth over her back, across her shoulders. He lifted her hair to wipe her nape. Next, he lightly daubed her heated butt cheeks. She'd never been much for aftercare, preferring her own company and shower, but this felt luxurious.

"Shouldn't have any marks tomorrow from my belt."

"Then maybe you should have used it a little harder." She looked back at him. His eyes were narrowed, and she wondered for a second if she'd gone too far. "I would love to see it in the mirror tomorrow as a reminder."

"You are adventurous."

"I think you knew that from the beginning, Sir."

"Yeah. I did."

"So are you going to fuck me?" She lifted her wrists as much as the rope would allow. "Or is this goodnight?" she asked, repeating his earlier question.

He wadded the washcloth then threw it, and she saw it land near his discarded shirt. He'd already tossed aside his belt. As she watched, transfixed, he unfastened the metal button at his waist then lowered the zipper on his jeans.

He was already fully erect, and she was surprised that he didn't wear any underwear. "Commando, Sir?" He didn't seem the type. She'd expected tighty-whiteys or, at the least, boxers. Perhaps unfairly, but she'd judged him to be a bit staid, too polite. In all her years of playing with various people in the lifestyle, she'd never come across anyone like him.

She had another surprise after he toed off his boots, pulled off his socks and lowered his jeans. His balls were shaved, and he only had a small patch of closely trimmed pubic hair. "You, Sir, are totally hot." Her rear and the backs of her thighs still felt seared. She was beginning to notice the ache in her nipples again. The clamps hadn't bothered her while he was playing with her, but now she was beginning to feel real discomfort. If he didn't give her some attention soon, she'd crawl out of her skin.

He stroked his dick a couple of times.

"You were serious that you want to torment me."

"Both of us," he said.

He opened a drawer and removed a condom. He ripped it open and placed it on his cockhead. "Your turn," he said.

"Sir?"

"Roll it down me."

"Are you serious, Sir? My hands are tied."

"Use your mouth."

"I've never done that before."

"Happy to be your first."

No doubt she'd underestimated him. He knelt on the bed and took hold of her head, cradling it between his strong palms, offering support, but also giving her no chance to pull away.

She opened her mouth and tentatively closed it around him. Since she was somewhat perplexed about how to actually accomplish his task, her motions were awkward. Still, this felt extraordinarily erotic, and the idea of pleasing him made her giddy. He massaged her scalp as she worked, and he offered no criticism.

"You're doing well," he said, as she used her tongue to work the latex past his cockhead.

For a moment, she pressed the tip of her tongue against the spot under his shaft where she knew he would be the most sensitive.

He tightened his grip on her head. Encouraged, she drew her mouth up a bit then went down again, unrolling the condom a little farther.

"Maybe this wasn't such a good idea," he said.

She wished her hands were free, but she gamely continued to try to figure it out, using only gentle pressure from her teeth as she worked the latex into place. Knowing it was driving him mad helped her enjoy it more, and she took extra time on the areas where he involuntarily moved his hips.

She turned her head sideways to lick the underside of his dick as if it were an ice cream cone. His cock thickened and she increased her tempo.

"Enough," he finally said, the word nearly a growl. He pulled her head away.

She looked up at him.

Her in-control, take-charge Dom had his jaw clenched. His rich green eyes were narrowed, and she was reminded of a shard of jade. She smiled. It hadn't taken her long to bring him to the brink. "I was just getting the hang of it, Sir."

"Oh, I want a blow job from you, and no doubt it will be world class, but now is not the time." He tugged on the chain running between her clamps.

She jerked upright at the sudden burn. "Sir!" It had taken only seconds for him to take control.

"Let's get you back in position."

He picked her up and moved her back onto her knees. "Forehead on the mattress." He made sure she was balanced then checked that the rope wasn't chafing bare skin.

In this position, her breasts weren't pressed against the bed, and she was grateful for that small mercy.

"I've been fantasising all night about having my hand in your hair as I fuck you from behind."

The image filled her mind, obliterating all thoughts.

"And I'm going to put a finger up your ass."

He hadn't phrased it as a request. She knew she could refuse, but the idea had a wicked appeal to her.

He put the bottle of lube on the sheet then moved behind her.

Simultaneously, he slapped both of her ass cheeks.

The unexpected blow shocked her. She might have toppled over, but he was there, his hands on her waist, steadying her. "Damn, Sir." The momentary explosion of pain receded, lancing her with arousal.

Because he'd spanked her earlier, the feeling seemed magnified.

"Are you getting ready for me, Sydney?"

"More," she said.

"More of what?"

She thrust her hips back towards him in silent plea.

Thankfully he didn't make her beg. "That's a good little subbie," he said.

He tapped each cheek then hit her harder and harder still, tanning her hide the way she'd hoped would happen when she'd walked through the Den's front door earlier this evening.

She surrendered, allowing the blows to rain randomly across her bare cheeks and thighs.

It went on and on, and she started to get lost in her head. Her breaths were no longer shallow. They were longer, farther apart. She felt only pleasure. Nothing existed but the sensual connection of skin on skin.

Before she was ready, he was rubbing her scorched rear.

"Are you with me, Sydney?"

His voice sounded gruff and distant. He placed both his hands on her back, grounding her. "Yes, Sir," she said obediently.

"Your responses are perfect."

"No, Sir. It's you." She meant his treatment of her was the perfect thing, and she hoped he understood that because her tongue suddenly felt too big for her mouth.

She felt him part her buttocks.

"Lift your butt higher, little sub."

She manoeuvred, but the position forced her breasts down. His ass-warming had distracted her from the discomfort and now she was hyperaware of it again. After tonight, she might choose never to wear the clamps again. But the way he'd removed them from her earlier had made everything bearable. She'd loved having him suck her nipples.

He played with her pussy, his motions turning her on, making her slicker. The delicious blows had already prepared her pussy for him.

Master Michael placed the tip of his cock against her cunt and began to ease his way inside. She sucked in a breath. He pulled back after the first couple of shallow strokes, driving her mad. "Sir!"

"So wet," he said. "Patience."

He might as well have asked the earth to stop spinning. She arched her back, trying to encourage him along, but this confounding man moved at his own pace. She told herself not to be frustrated—after all, he'd made sure their time together was memorable—but damn, she was ready to have his entire cock in her.

"Give up the struggle."

She twisted her fingers together. Since she had no other choice, she tried to school her mind.

He rocked his pelvis, going deeper with each thrust.

Sydney forced her fingers apart. And when she took his advice, the slow fuck became more enjoyable.

"That's it," he said.

She became aware of all the sensations, the way he filled her and his girth stretched her. His work-hewn hands were on her buttocks still, keeping the globes parted. His motions slid her breasts back and forth on the mattress, and the resulting pain seemed to shoot straight to her pussy. On its journey it seemed to transform into pleasure, and she felt an orgasm beginning to form. "Sir, I think I'm going to come."

"Do," he told her, his voice wrapping around her. "From here forward, you don't need permission."

His earlier denial made his change of heart more empowering. She felt as if she'd been untethered. Clearly this man was more of an expert than she'd realised.

He continued his unhurried pace.

It was enough.

She arched her back more, flattening her breasts, and offering herself to him. He sank in deep, and he moved his grip to her hip bones, holding her in place.

"Come," he whispered. He pulled back then surged forwards.

She cried out as the orgasm pulsed through her pussy.

"Ride it," he told her.

She shuddered against him, prolonging the thrill.

"That's it," he approved.

Once the shocks had subsided, she heard the sound of something wet, and she suspected he'd squirted out a dollop of lube. Reflexively she squeezed her lower body. Then she felt something wet and cold against her anus.

"Open up."

She drummed her fingers helplessly on the bed.

"I mean it."

He reached over and gave a quick tug on the chain of her nipple clamps.

The bastard took advantage of her shift to insert the tip of his finger in her rectum. "It will be better than you're expecting," he promised.

She wasn't anticipating she'd like it at all. In fact, she was certain she wouldn't.

The man was relentless in his pursuit of what he wanted. He moved his left arm beneath her hip bones to support her weight as he put his cock in her. As he filled her cunt, he moved his finger in and out of her rear.

She felt overfull. Because he was also finger-fucking her ass, she seemed smaller, the fit impossibly tight.

"Imagine what it will be like when you have a fat plug there."

She shook her head. "No, Sir."

He laughed. "I love it when you tell me no, little sub."

Despite her reservations, she succumbed to him. Her temporary Dom put a finger all the way up her, seating it to the knuckle. She gasped.

He began to fuck her with it, twisting his finger as he pushed in.

It wasn't nearly as bad as she'd feared it would be. And within less than a minute, her normal thirst to experience something new had reasserted itself.

"What do you think, Sydney?" Instead of waiting for a response, he did her, hard.

Pain from the clamps combined with the forbidden thrill of the anal penetration and the pounding from his thick dick created a plethora of excitement she'd never felt before. He left her breathless.

She cried out an orgasm, but he kept going, never acknowledging it by slowing down. As a Dom, he overwhelmed her. She was grateful for his arm beneath her, supporting her since she wasn't sure she could have held herself up.

She'd thought the orgasms up until now had been exquisite, but this was beyond anything she'd hoped for.

"Damn," he muttered. "So, so good."

Then he was at her rear again, forcing her sphincter wider as he added a second finger. "I can't," she protested.

"You can. You will."

She did, and she was grateful for it. Going beyond her self-imposed limits was more incredible than she'd thought possible.

He continued his relentless onslaught, and she came again and again. She felt as if she were having an out of body experience.

It seemed an incredible amount of time later when she felt a change in his rhythm. A sense of feminine power crept over her when he gave a guttural moan. "Come, Sir," she said. "Deep in me. Give it to me."

With the arm he had beneath her, he powerfully lifted her lower body off the mattress, owning her as he gave a final few jerky motions before pulsing inside her.

"So hot, Sir."

"Fuck," he muttered.

She felt him convulse and she smiled, wondering who dominated whom.

He held her for several moments before easing his fingers from her. Her heartbeat started to return to normal. Eventually she exhaled a shaky breath. "Well, Sir..." She left the sentence unfinished as she had no words.

"Stay as you are," he said, withdrawing by slow measures.

Before she had fully realised that he was gone, she heard water running in the en suite. He was back right away with a washcloth to cleanse her. Then he pressed the warm towel against her rear, soothing the ache there.

"Let's get you untied."

"How about the clamps, Sir?"

"We'll do those last."

She started to protest. Then, recognising it would do no good anyway, she shut her mouth.

His motions were deft as he loosened the scarves around her wrists. "I don't know," he said, pausing. "I like having you like this with your ass presented so prettily. Maybe I'll keep you fastened like this."

"Beast."

"Excuse me?"

"Beast, *Sir.*"

He chuckled, proving he'd taken no offence.

The scarves fell away as he moved her onto her back. "Now the clamps," he said.

She met his gaze. The man was sinfully handsome, his face all hard angles, and he looked serious as he studied her.

He took hold of the chain and yanked.

The pain sizzled and she whimpered. He placed a hand on her cunt, gave her a hard slap, then masturbated her to another completion. "God, God, God!" she screamed.

"I like the unexpected as much as you do," he said.

She narrowed her eyes at him.

"You can thank me at any time."

"Thank you, Sir," she said. She even meant it. She had figured his climax had signalled the end of their encounter, so the additional orgasm left her dazed. She shuddered on her next breath.

He sat next to her to remove the clamps. She appreciated the paradox of him. Big and strong, but gentle and caring. He was devastatingly handsome with those bright green eyes that missed nothing.

Like he had earlier, he alleviated the anguish of the blood rushing back into her nipples by immediately putting his mouth on her flesh and gently sucking. "Thank you for your consideration, Sir."

"I'll always take care of you, Sydney." He dropped the clamps on the nightstand. "Would you like a shower?"

She hesitated. This was the moment she'd dreaded. They both knew he wasn't just asking if she wanted a shower. He was inviting her to stay. She wasn't big on the morning after. Yet she was reluctant to leave him.

Patiently he waited, never pushing her.

Her answer surprised her. "Yes, I think I would. Thank you, Sir."

"I was hoping you'd say that."

Before she could respond, he scooped her from the bed.

"I can walk," she protested, but the words sounded weak, even to her.

"No doubt."

Other than that, he didn't acknowledge that she'd spoken. He carried her into the master bathroom. "Good grief," she exclaimed when he placed her on the tiled floor. "This isn't what I expected."

"I took out a bedroom so I could have a little space."

"A little space?" she repeated, looking around. "I've stayed in hotel rooms smaller than this. Recently, even." Though it was huge, it was still in keeping with the rest of the house. Thin planks of aspen or pine—she wasn't sure which—angled across the walls. A sandstone vanity had dual sinks with wall-mounted faucets. The room had several mirrors, one full-length. An oval-shaped princess-looking mirror above a sink actually tilted.

Wooden shelves held thick towels and even a few candles. A large shower unit was tiled in glass. The focal point of the room was a picture window that dominated the space above a soaker tub. "Do you bring a lot of women here?" she asked. It bothered her how much his answer suddenly mattered.

"The tub is for me. I work on the ranch. Nothing better for sore muscles."

"You didn't answer my question."

He folded his arms across his chest.

It struck her how odd the situation was. This was precisely why she preferred to scene at the Den, then dress and go home. Saying goodbye right away avoided any awkwardness. She wasn't looking for anything other than a thrilling ride.

This man, despite the fact that his behaviour was atypical, was still a Dom. If she were smart, she'd leave now. Instead, she stood there, looking at him, admiring his tattoo. In the bright light she noticed a number of scars on his body, including a jagged one that cut diagonally beneath his ribs.

He was handsome, and he'd given her more, much, much more than any man she'd been with, even the one who'd collared her. His cock, she noticed, was partially hard, and that made her wonder what else they could share sexually.

"I'm not very good at this submissive thing," she said.

"I'm not very good at the vanilla thing," he replied.

"Stalemate. I should go." Her heart sped up.

He took a step to the side. "I won't stop you. Ever."

She reached for one of the huge white towels and wrapped herself in it. It was the size of a small sheet. "Damn it." She didn't want it to end on this note. How was she screwing it up so badly?

"It's a long drive back."

"Could I just stay as a guest?"

He didn't give her a direct answer. That would have been too simple, and he was anything but.

"There's a reason I rarely date," he said. "After my divorce, I decided I would be blunt about my expectations. My woman, whoever she is, will know the rules and abide by them. I've been very clear with you."

"You have."

"But in answer to your question, Sydney, you're the first one I've invited to spend the night." He stayed where he was, continuing to give her space. "I'd like it if you accepted my invitation, but as I said, the choice is yours. If you want to leave but don't want to drive alone, I can take you or one of my wranglers will. There's also a guest room you're welcome to use. But if you're in my bedroom, you're my sub."

The fight went out of her. "I…" She faced the truth. She didn't want to leave. But she didn't want to be a sub, either. It hadn't worked well for her with Lewis. Yet the two men couldn't be any more different. Which wasn't exactly a comfort. Master Michael was a far bigger threat to her individuality than Lewis could have ever been. And that was the conundrum.

"It's not a lifetime commitment," he said wryly. "It's only a few hours."

"You're right. I suppose I could try it, for one night."

"Generous of you."

"There was no insult meant, Sir."

"Would you like me to run you a bath or start the shower?"

She frowned at him. Although she was covered from chest to toe, his size and nakedness intimidated her. "How does that fit in with being a sub?"

"You could wash my back."

She started to smile, but she wasn't sure whether or not he was teasing.

"Look, Sydney, we don't know each other that well. We can figure it out together, or not. Your choice. I would like you to stay. If you do, I expect you to behave submissively."

When she started to argue, he lifted a large hand to stop her. "We can define what that means. I don't anticipate you'll stop being who you are. I demand respect, courtesy and communication. Lack of it will be discussed then dealt with swiftly."

A chill enveloped her. Secretly, she wondered if she had been looking for something like this. She'd been young when she'd entered the relationship with Lewis. In his way, he'd been as young as her, and the relationship had been as quirky was it had been kinky. She hadn't known much about lifestyle BDSM, and neither had he. Studded collars, dog leashes and tight latex for both of them had made up their weekend outings.

Master Michael was different, a rugged individual who seemed to have some rigid expectations. Being with him was unique. It might be a novelty that would wear off quickly, like having too much cotton candy at the fair. "I hate giving in," she admitted.

"Then yield instead."

"Sir?"

"Get your ass in the shower, Sydney, before I use that back scrubber as a paddle."

The long piece of wood hung from a peg in the shower stall. The implement looked like an oversized hairbrush and it had definite potential for a harsh spanking.

"Right, then," he said.

Her mouth fell open.

He opened the glass door and grabbed the scrubber. "Bend over the bathtub."

"Are you serious?"

He smacked the back end of it against his left palm. She jumped.

"Bend over the bathtub," he repeated. "Drop the towel."

"My butt is already sore, Sir."

"And the longer you wait, the worse it will be."

She debated using a safe word, but she wanted it. And he knew it. Sydney took her time untucking the towel and letting it fall to the tiles. She turned away to move into place.

"Wait."

"Sir?" She faced him.

His eyes had a gleam she didn't recognise. A part of her was frightened. A bigger part of her made her stand her ground.

"Spread your legs." He moved his hand much lower on the handle and turned over the scrubber so the bristles pointed up.

"Oh, no. No way." She shook her head. "Absolutely not, Sir."

"*Tur-tle?*" He broke the word into two syllables — on purpose, she was sure, returning her earlier goading. "Spread your legs and put your hands behind your neck."

She looked at the pokey points then at his face.

She didn't see anything malicious there. His eyes appeared a shade lighter than they had earlier. It could be because of the brilliant light. Or it could be because of his dare. Either way, she did as he demanded.

"Don't hump it like a naughty little subbie."

"As if, Sir." She kept her head tipped back so she could look at him.

He dropped his gaze to her crotch.

She gulped as he touched the bristles to her tender pussy. For the first time, she wasn't sure she could go through with something.

His touch was achingly gentle as he went back and forth.

"Oh," she said. Despite her trepidation, she liked this. She rose up, giving him greater access.

"I hope you learn to trust me," he said, his mouth near her ear.

He exerted a small amount of pressure but continued to move with exquisite slowness. An orgasm teased her, remaining just out of reach. "I think I could come," she said.

"What do you need for that to happen?"

"Maybe a little more stimulation."

"Before or after the strokes on your ass?"

"Sir! This isn't instead of a spanking?"

"No," he said. He reached his free hand between her legs and spread her labia. "This is in addition to the spanking. Like whipped cream with an Irish coffee."

At his increased pressure, she slammed her heels onto the floor. "Yow, Sir!"

"Come any time."

She leant forwards into him, and he adjusted his stance to support her. Lost, she closed her eyes. Everything tingled. She bent her knees and rocked.

"You are humping it, you naughty sub."

She was gone. Trembling, she climaxed.

He moved without her realising it, wrapping an arm around her waist.

"You're an insatiable wench."

"Sorry, Sir."

"Don't ever apologise for that," he said.

He pulled the brush away. Her skin seemed aflame, but in the most fabulous way. Before she was thinking straight, he walked her a few steps to the side of the bathtub. "Hold on," he told her. "Keep your knees together. I'm going to start just above your knees and work my way up. If you need to flex, do so, but as soon as you can compose yourself, resume the position I specified."

Fighting the delirium, she braced herself.

"Repeat what I said."

She looked over her shoulder. He fingered back her hair, tucking the strands behind her ears. "You said, Sir, that I should keep my legs together." How could he be so perfect? There was a tenderness in his tone that was at odds with his stance and the fact that he held the punishing wooden brush. "You'll start at the bottom and work your way up. If I get out of position, I should get back in as soon as I can."

"Close enough." He lowered his hand.

The first spank seared. The second was a lot more powerful. The third, on a fleshier part of her leg, was higher and harder.

He knew...how to give her what she wanted. How to inflict pain with deliberate intensity. How to keep her guessing.

The one on the underneath of her buttocks forced her to lift up. She closed her eyes, waited for the pain to settle then re-gripped the tub. While he wasn't letting her be in charge, he allowed her to set the pace.

"Last one."

She tightened her cheeks, expecting it to blaze. She waited and waited. But it didn't come. Finally, it dawned on her. He was waiting.

With great determination, she loosened her muscles. Only then did he lay the brush to her.

She sucked a breath through her teeth.

"Now your ass is a pretty shade of pink."

"It matches my pussy then, Sir."

"So it does." He helped her stand and turn around. "Cool shower or a warm one?"

"One without bristles," she said, dubiously eyeing the brush.

"Shouldn't have said that. I may keep one in every room."

She considered a snappy comeback then thought better of it. Her rear felt hot. She wouldn't survive another beating. And she wouldn't put it past him to give her one.

He moved across the bathroom to turn on the shower. After checking the temperature twice, he looked at her calculatingly before lowering the adjustable showerhead. "Your shower, madame. Feel free to use anything in there."

"This is luxurious," she said stepped into the oversized glass enclosure. At her condo, the fixture was small and attached to the wall above the tile. She spent most of her time moving around beneath the pelting water, trying to rinse off soap or shampoo, and getting a chill wherever the uneven spray wasn't hitting.

"Can I scrub your back?" he offered.

"Hell, no," she muttered.

"I didn't quite hear you."

That had been her intention. "I said this is perfect as it is, Sir."

"That's what I thought."

Steam billowed in the stall. She watched him move around the bathroom, clearly comfortable with his nakedness.

"Washcloth?"

"Yes, please."

He handed one in, along with a fresh bar of soap.

"I figured you'd want something unscented."

"Thanks." She wasn't sure she'd ever been in the same bathroom with a man before. When she and Lewis had cohabitated, she'd taken over the guest bathroom. But this man, apparently, didn't believe in giving or expecting privacy. The thought unnerved her. She'd do well to leave as early as possible in the morning.

He draped a towel over the top of the glass door. Did he think of everything?

When he left the bathroom, she sighed and hurriedly washed herself. She was grateful he'd given her this bar. It was bad enough that she'd be sleeping next to him, inhaling his masculine scent. If she used his soap, at least a hint would remain on her skin even after they parted. And the last thing she needed was to be going out of her mind with reminders of him.

She used his shampoo and wished he had conditioner. The outdoor spanking followed by him wrapping his hand in her hair had made a mess of her locks. It would take days to detangle it all.

After reluctantly turning off the shower, she wrapped herself in a towel. He'd left an unopened toothbrush on the counter. It was scary what an exceptional host he was.

In the bedroom, he'd put away the toy box, arranged the pillows and pulled up a blanket. And he was still distractingly naked. As he drew the blinds he told her, "I'm going to take a quick shower."

"Do you have a T-shirt I can borrow, Sir?" Anything of his would swallow her, and she liked that idea.

"You won't need one. I'll keep you warm."

"I don't like to sleep nude."

"Because?"

"I was in a hotel in Belize that was evacuated in the middle of the night, so I've learnt to wear something to bed."

"Sounds reasonable."

"So, can I borrow a T-shirt?"

"No. But I'm willing to compromise. I'll get you a T-shirt, and you can hang it on the bedpost. If you wake up cold or if we have a fire, it will be right there."

She sighed. "There's no dissuading you when you've made a decision, is there?"

"If you wanted to be with a man you could push around, you wouldn't have come home with me."

"That's a warped kind of logic, Sir."

"Regardless, I'm right." Without another word, he headed into the bathroom.

She watched him go. She couldn't remember having been around a man so confounding, frustrating...and, damn it, intriguing.

He left the door open, and she heard water running. No. He definitely didn't believe in privacy. But after all they'd already shared, what was left?

She used the towel to squeeze excess water from her hair then finger-combed the strands the best she could. There was a brush in the console of her car, along with a bag filled with extra clothes, a pair of hiking boots and some toiletries. She'd been known to take impromptu trips, and once, while she'd been walking across a river in Wyoming, she'd slipped off a rock and fallen in the icy water. Having extra clothes and shoes had been a lifesaver.

Sudden silence filled the house, meaning he'd turned off the shower. Now she really couldn't make an escape, not that she'd really wanted to in the dark, with only a leather dress and high heels to slip into.

Less than thirty seconds later, he entered the bedroom with a towel wrapped around his waist. His hair was damp, making it look darker, and a few drops of water clung to his chest.

How was it possible that he'd satisfied her so completely and she was ravenous again?

"Drop it," he said, nodding towards her towel. "Please," he added, disarming her. He smiled.

Damn him. She was lost. She might have protested his command, but his smile was impossible to resist.

"You'll be lucky if I ever let you wear clothes again," he said when the material landed on the floor.

He snatched it up and carried it into the closet. When he returned, he'd discarded his towel as well. He held a black T-shirt, which he hung on the bedpost as promised. "Which side do you want?" he asked.

"The one closest to the door."

"Of course," he said. He climbed into bed and said, "Come here."

She hadn't spent the night with anyone since Lewis.

"I bite," he promised.

"It's a deal." He *did* know her. If he could make her smile, he would win.

She climbed into bed next to him. "I don't snuggle," she warned him, hugging the edge of the mattress.

"*Didn't*," he corrected, dragging her back against him and holding her tight. "You didn't snuggle. Now you do."

Master Michael was hard and unyielding, complex, yet transparent. He didn't play games. He was blunt about what he expected. It seemed he was willing to negotiate and soothe her if it made sense, but if he believed she was being unreasonable, he'd state his case and wait for her capitulation.

In his arms, she felt safe and protected. That thought made her stiffen her body. She had been on her own since she was young, and she didn't need to lean on anyone.

"Stop your struggle, little sub."

He moved so that he could position his semi-erect cock between her buttocks. His thighs were against the backs of her legs, and he held her tight.

It had been a hell of a night.

A coyote howled in the distance. She knew she'd never feel at ease, let alone actually sleep, but, shocking her, the next thing she knew, the watery light of predawn was filtering through the slats in the window blinds.

She hated to admit that he'd been right. He'd kept her warm all night. Needing a few minutes to herself to sort through her turbulent emotions, she eased herself away from him.

"Sub," he mumbled. "Stay."

"I'm not leaving," she promised with a whisper. Unable to help herself, she turned and eased a curled lock of light brown hair back from his forehead. Last night, she hadn't had time to really look at him.

He appeared so different in the daylight, and in sleep. His brow was relaxed. She noticed the rough planes and angles. His skin was dark from the Colorado sun, but the tiny lines grooved next to his eyes were less pronounced. His lips were slightly parted.

A jolt went through her when she remembered what he'd done to her with that mouth last night. That thought was quickly followed by the realisation he'd exerted a dominant power over her that no one else ever had.

Restless, she climbed from the bed.

She reached for the T-shirt hanging from the bedpost then saw his discarded long-sleeved shirt on the floor. She picked that up instead.

At the doorway, she paused, glancing back at him. She thought he might have one eye open slightly then decided that wasn't case. If he had been aware she was leaving the bed, she doubted he'd have let her go.

So as not to disturb him, she tiptoed down the stairs. Sydney exercised every day, yet her muscles ached. He'd kept her in odd positions for hours. But she didn't regret it.

Downstairs, she used the small powder room. In the mirror she noticed a few serious-looking stripes on the backs of her thighs. She traced one with her fingertip. He had, no doubt, given her what she'd asked for. Generally, the morning after she resumed her normal life. The night before was almost never worth replaying in her head.

But this…

She made her way to the kitchen, passing her shoes that had somehow ended up near opposite walls. Her dress was draped over a chair back, but she had no recollection of having taken that much care with it. Had he?

Her head felt as if it had been stuffed with cotton.

In the kitchen she found the coffee pot and a pound of ground beans. She grabbed the bag, surprised to note the addition of chicory. Though she'd had it in a café au lait at a small place near the Mississippi river when she'd visited New Orleans, she'd never seen anyone out West drink it. But it suited him. It was an acquired taste, softening a dark roast, but adding a hint of chocolate flavour. As she tried to figure out how much to shake into the basket filter, she wondered how many more surprises he had in store for her.

She watched the brewer spit into the pot and wished he had a single-serve unit like she had at home. Since she didn't have the patience to watch it hiss and splat, she rooted through the cabinets until she found a cup she could carry outside. Then, tired of waiting, she pulled out the carafe and filled her cup.

Now she knew why it was usually served mixed with half a cup of steamed milk. She found a half-gallon bottle of unopened milk in his refrigerator. There wasn't a single container of anything with hazelnut or vanilla like she preferred. She prised the lid off the glass bottle and almost swooned at the sight of the pure cream on the top. For a moment—well, less than a moment—she debated saving the treasure for him. But then she greedily poured it into her cup.

She hadn't seen something like that since she'd been overseas as a child. Ranch living clearly had some advantages.

Fortified with her coffee, she slipped into her shoes and headed for the front door. The morning sunlight blazed down, unobstructed by a single cloud. She saw the land in a way she'd missed last night. Off to the left were several buildings. One looked like a barn, but others she didn't recognise. A corral was in the distance, though she didn't see any horses.

In front of her, a vista swept out to distant mountain peaks, some over twelve thousand feet tall, a few soaring higher than thirteen thousand feet.

She called the picturesque town of Evergreen home and had travelled all of her life, but this sight took her breath away as nothing else had. The adventurer in her wanted to explore. A walk would definitely be good for her unsettled mind.

She made her way down the path and wondered how she hadn't twisted an ankle last night. Without Master Michael's assistance, she would never have made it.

She opened the gate and delicately picked her way through the dirt and gravel to her car. After taking a sip of the welcome and strong coffee, with the stolen cream, she placed her cup on the roof then opened the back door and reached in for her duffel bag.

She'd just curled her hand around the strap when she was shoved from behind, sending her sprawling across the back seat. She screamed and instantly reacted, shoving herself backwards and turning, ready to fight, either Master Michael or someone else. He'd mentioned having ranch hands, hadn't he?

Her heart thundered.

No one was there.

Then she heard a pitiful bleat.

She looked down to see the smallest goat imaginable. It looked like a baby. A kid, or whatever young goats were called. Then she recalled Master Michael telling her it was some sort of miniature.

Closing her eyes, she exhaled. She collapsed against the side of the vehicle, trying to steady her racing heart. Embarrassed, Sydney looked around to make sure no one had witnessed her attempt at self-defence against an undersized mammal. The stilettos and man's shirt added layers to the pile of humiliation.

The thing cocked its head to the side and bleated again. "Nice goat," she said, pushing herself away from the car, crisis over.

It moved in again. "Uh..." It butted her hand then looked up at her with wide, unblinking eyes.

Good God. She was being imprisoned by a tiny terrorist.

She didn't know much—strike that, she knew *nothing*—about four-footed animals. Since it wouldn't have fitted her parents' lifestyle, she'd never been allowed to have pets, not even a goldfish.

She tried to take a step, but it surged forward again. "Look, you little creature, back off."

It did, but only long enough to ram her again.

At a loss, she reached out and touched its head.

It gave another bleat, but this sounded a bit different, a higher pitch.

Looking around, hoping for someone to rescue her, she scratched behind its ear. She'd seen a friend do that to an obnoxious dog once. The goat turned its head, giving her better access. Then it made a ridiculous noise, like a laugh. *Who knew it could do that?*

"Shouldn't you be in a pen or something, rather than wandering around?" It shoved its head at her again, evidently because she'd stopped petting it. Sydney wondered if things could be any more bizarre.

Not quite as intimidated, she manoeuvred until she could climb back into the vehicle. The tiny little thing tried to follow her. She was suddenly nervous again. She used one foot to gently push it down. But her shoe came loose and the thief absconded with it. "Damn it! Bring that back!"

He—or she—dropped it. Then it laughed, picked up her shoe and high-tailed it out of there. Suddenly, Sydney remembered Master Michael telling her the beast's name was Chewie. "Get back here!" she called. She exhaled in exasperation when it kept moving.

Ranching, she decided, cream or no cream in her coffee, wasn't for her.

She hurriedly grabbed a pair of lightweight hiking pants from her bag, worked her way into them then pulled on some socks and boots.

After tossing the remaining shoe forlornly in the bag, she went after the midget. The thing was nowhere to be found. "Damn it."

Trying to pretend the shoes hadn't cost a week's wages, she set out at a brisk pace towards the river.

The walk helped burn off some of the frustration. Some of her friends used yoga or breathing to calm themselves. For her, being out of breath was the only thing that worked. Scaling a mountain was significantly more helpful to her than a day at the spa.

The irritation returned when she remembered she'd left the coffee cup on top of the car.

Rather than going back for it, she allowed the sound of water to lure her.

As she stood at the edge, watching the river rush over rocks, she saw an eagle overhead. She watched it for long minutes as it caught thermals, soaring with hardly a flap. She could get used to it out here.

At least that's what she thought until she heard a familiar and unwelcome bleat. The goat emerged from between two pine trees. And it didn't have her shoe. "You're a pest." She sat and Chewie lowered himself onto his knees next to her. "I was enjoying this until you showed up," she told the thing.

It blinked.

"Fine. You can stay. But I want my shoe back."

It shook its head, but Sydney knew the timing was an odd coincidence.

She stayed where she was for longer than she could remember, and she finally gave in and stroked its spiny back. The short fur—or was it hair?—was softer than she'd thought it would be. The black and white creature had a few small brown markings and was surprisingly adorable, despite its bad manners. "Don't get any ideas," she said. "I mean it. Stop looking at me like that."

Chewie bumped her hand, its ears standing straight up.

"You forgot this."

She jumped at the sound of Master Michael's voice. How had she not heard his approach? With a half-smile, she looked over her shoulder to see him standing there holding two cups of coffee. "Bless you," she said.

The goat abandoned her and went straight to him. Clearly even the goat knew who the master was.

He crouched next to her and offered her the same cup she'd abandoned on top of the car. As their hands connected, she glanced away. He had on his requisite hat and a long-sleeved shirt much like the one she'd donned. He'd rolled back the cuffs, leaving his forearms bare. Faded denim jeans conformed to his muscular legs. Despite the summer day, he looked like a working man.

"I see you've met Chewie."

"And lost a favourite shoe," she said wryly.

"Expensive?"

"Yes."

He winced. "I'll replace them."

"*Very* expensive," she amended. Then unable to help herself, she laughed. "I don't wear them all that often. I have others."

"I've seen some with spikes on the heels. They were red, as I recall."

"I like red."

"They'd look good on you."

She brought her knees to her chest and wrapped her arms around them. "Maybe I will take you up on your offer."

"You should."

Chewie wandered down to the water for a drink.

"And I'll take you up on yours," he said.

Though his tone was still light, she heard a serious undercurrent. She took a sip of the still warm and very much welcome coffee and looked at him. "Sir?"

"The one where you get on your knees and suck my cock in apology for leaving my bed without permission."

She jerked her hand, sloshing the coffee. "Ah…"

He took the cup from her hand and placed it on the ground. "Or the one where you pull down your pants, lie across my lap and beg me to punish you for the same reason."

Breath constricted in her chest. A serious line was drawn between his eyebrows. With a squeak, she managed, "Here? Now?"

"Or the one where I tie you to the fence and flog you."

This man aroused her with only his words. "Do I have to choose one? Or can I select all of the above?"

Chapter Five

"I'm always happy to accommodate a beautiful little sub," he said.

She opened her eyes wide. Apparently his response had caught her off guard. No doubt other men tripped over their tongues at her sass, using that as an excuse to dole out the beatings she'd searched out. No doubt her cloak of invincibility had been polished to perfection. And it was likely useful for keeping most men away. She affected an air of nonchalance from the confidence in her stride, the way she held her shoulders back, even the flip of her hair.

Despite Gregorio's warning, or maybe because of it, Michael had looked past her perfect hair and makeup, form-fitting leather dress, fuck-me heels and attitude, searching for the vulnerable woman beneath. Watching her, he continued, "Which order would you like to go in? First to last? Or last to first?" he asked. "Or, we could start with the second option. Having your body pressed against my cock will get me hard, saving you a few seconds on the blow job."

He'd be willing to bet she had no idea how expressive her face was. When something intrigued her, she parted her lips. Her breathing also changed, becoming faster. And that made him want her even more.

Seeing her here, now, in her natural state, wearing baggy nylon pants and sturdy boots, with hair ravaged, no makeup and dressed in one of his shirts, she had no artifice.

Earlier, when she'd touched his face in bed, he'd considered letting her know he was awake. He was a notoriously light sleeper, aware of every noise inside and outside the house. But the opportunity to observe Sydney's unguarded moments had been irresistible, despite the hard-on urging him to grab her, pin her beneath him and slake his morning lust.

He'd heard her moving about the kitchen then smelt the aroma of brewing coffee. He'd taken his time pulling on a pair of jeans and a T-shirt. But before he'd made it down the stairs, he'd heard the front door close. He'd noticed her leather dress was still artfully draped across a chair, and her purse sat on the counter where she'd left it, so he wasn't concerned that she was leaving without saying goodbye.

Curious, though, he'd grabbed a cup of coffee. As a testament to how he felt about her, he hadn't even minded that she'd taken the cream from the top of the milk.

Barefoot, he'd wandered to the window. He'd enjoyed watching her interact with Chewie. He'd always figured he could learn a lot about a person based on the way they treated animals. Watching her tentatively reach out to pet the goat behind the ears had made him smile. Chewie was a decent judge of character, much like some dogs Michael had owned.

And the way she'd trotted along next to Sydney as they'd headed towards the river had told him a lot.

Taking his time, he'd headed upstairs to finish dressing. While he'd been putting on his clothes, he'd been mentally stripping hers off. Now he intended to do it in reality. "I want to kiss you," he said.

He put a hand in her hair and held the back of her head. He met her gaze, and he realised he could get lost in the blue depths of her eyes. They communicated her true emotion better than what came out of her mouth. If she knew he saw that, she'd be scared.

"Sir, I'd rather we just—"

"Sydney? Use a safe word or shut up." He prised apart her hands then pulled her between his legs. She was on her knees, and he was tugging her head back. He brushed his lips across hers. "Soft," he told her.

"Yes..."

This time, he licked her upper lip.

"That's sexy," she said.

He drew her bottom lip between his teeth and bit down with the slightest pressure.

She tipped back her chin.

"Open your mouth to me." He tightened his grip in her hair and yanked on the shirt to reveal her creamy chest.

She parted her lips, and he pressed his tongue to hers. She moaned from deep inside, and the slight sound of her capitulation galvanised him. He sought more, wanting her total surrender. She tasted of coffee, of morning, of promise.

He deepened the kiss and she responded, moving so she could wrap both her arms around him, knocking off his hat. Even if she wanted to hide who she really was, she was honest with her desires. He appreciated that, if nothing else.

She met each of his thrusts. He reached inside her shirt to caress one of her breasts, knowing she was probably tender. It wouldn't take much to arouse her, but he didn't want to make her too sore...yet. When he whipped her front later, he wanted her to enjoy the feel of deer hide biting at her nipples.

Boldly, she moved one hand lower and curled it over his growing cock. Now he wished he'd dressed in something other than jeans. He adjusted their positions, dragging her closer. She met his intensity with ferocity of her own. Still, he was in control, just as he should be.

By small measures he ended the kiss and eased his grip. "I should have done that last night. A dozen times last night," he amended.

"I don't normally kiss," she said.

"You do now."

"I suppose that's true, Sir. And since your hat seems to have fallen off..." She moved to press her palms against his chest. "We should get started on my offer." Diligently she set to work on his shirt, unfastening the buttons and pulling the hem from his waistband.

He let her lead. For now.

She shucked the material from his shoulders. She fumbled with the metal button of his jeans but continued until she released it. The zipper was another story. "I think your cock is making this more difficult," she said.

"What do you suggest?"

"Would you stand, please, Sir?"

He did.

She used both hands—one to hold the denim taut, the other to release the metal teeth. Then she tugged his jeans, letting them fall to his ankles. He removed his boots and jeans, and she knelt to take his cockhead in her mouth.

Without a condom, her tongue felt more amazing than it had last night.

She cupped his balls with one hand and stroked him with the other as she moved up and down his engorged shaft. She took him deep into her mouth until he was certain she was going to gag. But she didn't.

"Damn," he mumbled. Her touch was masterful. She placed a finger on his perineum and a million sensations zinged through him. He'd had blow jobs before, really good ones, but no one had been as dedicated to the task as she was.

She moved up and placed the tip of her tongue underneath his cock. She continued to move her hands quickly, tugging on his testicles, adding extra pressure to that sensitive spot near his anus and licking with the lightest of pressures.

Constantly she changed the tempo, licking and sucking harder as she used less pressure from her hands. Then she slid up and took his dick in her mouth again. She caressed, pulled, cupped, pressed. That she was into it, into him, drove him mad. "Sydney," he warned, on the verge.

She tightened her grip, driving his orgasm.

"Woman..." He moaned as ejaculate pulsed its way from his balls.

He expected her to pull away, maybe let him spill on the ground or her chest, but she didn't. She drew up, holding onto the tip of his cock as she swallowed it all. He put his hands on her head near her ears and she looked up. He wasn't sure how it was possible, but it appeared she was smiling while she still had him in her mouth. Finally, she let go, and she licked the last drop from the slit.

"Now I don't have to worry about your hard cock pressing against me while I get a spanking." She wiped tears from her face.

"Don't be too sure of that," he said, getting dressed again. "Come here."

He helped her to stand.

Since the ground was uneven, she took a hopping step to steady herself. He wrapped an arm around her waist then captured her chin and tilted her head back before gently brushing a kiss across her mouth. "Thank you."

"Thank you, Sir."

Michael heard Chewie bleat. He glanced over to see the caprine trotting off with his hat. Giving chase would make the Nigerian dwarf think he was playing a game. The best he could hope for was that he'd get it back without any pieces missing. He also knew he was a dreamer. "She thinks she's a dog, and she'll eat anything. Hyperactive hellion. I keep hoping she'll grow up."

"I guess my shoe is in good company."

"I should have hung it from a tree branch." He released her chin as he watched one of his most expensive hats bobbing up and down until it and the goat both disappeared.

"At least she didn't steal your pants."

He raised his brow. "Good point."

"But you could have covered the family jewels with your hat. Since you're flaccid, at least it wouldn't stick out." She snickered.

"You think that's funny?"

"Very, Sir."

"I think you do need that spanking."

Her smile widened.

"Incorrigible."

"Yes, Sir."

He spied a boulder. He took her hand and guided her towards it. "Drop your pants," he said, sitting and making sure the ground was solid beneath him so that his boot didn't accidentally slip, sending her sprawling. "You can hold one of my legs for balance since we're on an angle."

"Sir is very generous."

"Was that sarcasm, little sub?"

"Absolutely not, Sir. That would be disrespectful."

"Your pants," he reminded her. Her hand trembled slightly, delighting him. He loved that he had an effect on her. She had one on him. She draped herself over his knee. "Hard to decide which position I like you in the best."

"You always seem to have my ass sticking up."

"If you behaved better, maybe you wouldn't always need it warmed." He waited, cocking his head to the side. "No response?"

"Ah, that's not really incentive for me to behave, Sir." She kicked her legs a bit.

"Oh, right. The denied orgasm is most effective with you."

She stilled.

"You haven't been that bad, Sydney." Her reaction was interesting, though. She'd just reaffirmed that she feared emotional consequences over physical ones. That knowledge was good, and he'd use it judiciously. The woman was as fierce as she was attractive. Honestly, he appreciated her sharp wit. He understood why others might not. But he was clearly the winner. He had the delectable Sydney ready to squirm beneath his hand. "I couldn't be more pleased with you."

He reached between her legs, and she grabbed onto his left ankle. "Your pussy is already damp."

"It got wet while I was sucking you off, Sir."

His dick thickened at her words. No other woman had ever said as much. "I'm glad I ignored Gregorio's advice."

"I appreciate a man who's an independent thinker."

Her ass cheeks were still slightly red in parts, and he delighted in the opportunity to make the rest match. He brought his hand down on her buttocks.

"Ouch."

"More sarcasm?" He set his jaw. This woman calculated her words for maximum effect. He knew he'd need to call on all the reserves of patience he'd cultivated in his lifetime. She was probably hoping he'd lose control. He vowed he never would.

He aimed each of his next three rapid hits on the fleshiest part of her butt, taking care to avoid the parts that still bore welts. He paused to rub her vigorously, jostling her.

"Sir!"

"Hold on," he suggested.

He grabbed her buttocks and squeezed until she exhaled in an unladylike grunt. He eased off, but barely, before resuming a vigorous massage.

"That's... Shit!"

He slapped her hard, then fingered her. "Oh, you're even wetter. You're a perfect little sub."

"I'm not a —"

"You are. Mine. Now."

He tapped his foot, bouncing her around a bit. And he kept doing it as he resumed the spanking. He caught her a dozen times or more with his cupped hand, making her cry out. When she thrashed her legs, he teased her cunt again.

"Sir!"

He slapped her again and again. "Are you begging for mercy?" He could barely hear her response over her whimpers.

"Yes."

"Do you remember your safe and slow words?"

"I'm begging for an orgasm, Sir, not ever for you to stop!"

He chuckled. He'd been pretty sure that's what she'd meant.

Rapidly, he moved from hitting to squeezing, to teasing her swollen clit.

"Finger-fuck me, Sir."

Had she already learnt he could deny her nothing? He slipped a finger into her then he pulled some of the moisture backwards to lubricate her back hole.

She held her breath and tightened her muscles.

"That will not be tolerated." He placed two fingers in her pussy, gathering some more moisture. "Open up." He stroked her, encouraging her to lose the tension.

When she complied, he said, "That's a good girl."

He kept up what he was doing until she trembled, then he worked a finger inside her ass.

"Argh!"

"That's it." He adjusted himself to trap her legs. He upended her a little more in the process, forcing her to put one hand on the ground.

He moved rhythmically inside her then moved his other hand to spank her thighs. As she started to cry, he pressed a thumb against her clit and continued his relentless pounding of her rectum.

"Oh, Sir…"

"Come for me."

In an instant she did, clawing his pant leg, feverishly pumping her body. He encouraged her along until she went limp across him.

He offered soothing words, nonsensical words as he extracted his finger then helped her turn back over and sit up.

"That was... Christ, Sir. I feel scalded."

She didn't attempt to leave his knee. "That can only mean one thing. You need to cool off. In the river."

"Are you serious? I don't have a swimsuit."

"It's private."

"It's Colorado and the mountains. It's going to be cold."

"It will make your nipples stand up and beg for attention. That alone is reason enough for me. Don't tell me you've never skinny-dipped?"

"In a pool."

"But not in a river?"

She shook her head.

"You haven't lived. Scared?"

"I guide white water rafting tours. I've ended up in the water more than once."

"Then this should be nothing."

"It isn't."

But he saw he'd won. She'd accepted his challenge.

"What about that mangy pygmy—"

"Dwarf. She's a Nigerian dwarf goat," he told her for the second time. "And she's not mangy. She has regular baths, and she gets groomed often."

"She takes baths?"

He liked their easy banter, along with the fact that she seemed in no hurry to leave him. "I give them to her."

"You do?"

"My sister and the girls don't make it up here often, so I get the honours."

"You could braid her hair and tie it with ribbons and hang a blue ribbon around her neck and she'd still be a menace to society."

"Some females are," he agreed easily. "Present company excluded."

"Are you coming in with me?"

"Someone needs to twist your nipples."

"Ah..." She glanced around, looking at trees, and obviously checking to see if Chewie was around. "My clothes have to go somewhere. I can't have your pampered pet eating anything else of mine."

"So you're going in the water?"

"Yeah. It looks irresistible." She scampered off his lap and bent to pull off her hiking boots.

Obviously once she'd made up her mind, she didn't entertain second thoughts.

She peeled off her socks, shoved them in the boots then she tied the shoelaces together and looped them over a branch.

"Chewie can climb that rock." He pointed.

"She's a pain in the ass," Sydney said. She stood on tiptoe and selected a higher branch.

No matter how skilled or determined, the goat probably couldn't have reached the first location. He was sure she would try, but he was convinced she'd never succeed. But he was a red-blooded male and he'd wanted to watch Sydney stretch and rise up.

It didn't take her long to take off her remaining clothes, and she hung them on the tree, too.

Without waiting for him, she headed for the water's edge, picking her way over tiny rocks. He liked that she paused before getting in the river. Here it was fairly safe, not more than two feet deep. Spring run-off had ended and the land was all but flat.

Still, she looked upstream before surveying the downstream flow. Sydney was cautious yet brave, and not as reckless as her carefully cultivated reputation suggested. "There's a little pool area here where the water is almost still," she said. She crouched to stick her hand in the water. "It's not as cold as I expected."

He picked up his coffee and took a sip. Hell of a way to start the day, looking at a beautiful woman—a beautiful, *naked* woman, he amended. One who'd given him a hell of a blow job and whose ass had been reddened appropriately. He could get accustomed to having her around.

She entered the water by slow measures. "Damn!"

"Not that warm after all?"

"It is still only June, and it's early in the day," she said.

As he'd suspected, it barely came up to her knees.

"The shallow areas are quite different in temperature." She squatted, which was the only way to get herself wet up to the chest. Her nipples were tantalisingly erect when she stood and faced him. "Farther in, it's a bit colder. I thought you were coming in, Sir?"

He put their coffees on a rock before getting undressed.

Just as he'd watched her, she shamelessly studied him. Like she had done, he hung his clothes from pine tree branches.

"Nice butt, Sir."

Her voice held a seductive, feminine purr that turned him on.

He joined her, and before he adjusted to the shiver-inducing shock, the vixen splashed him. "You like to live dangerously."

"It was an accident, Sir."

"Uh-huh." The twinkling in her eyes said she was lying.

He joined his hands together, making a large cup, and he dunked them under the water. He stood and took a step towards her, droplets falling from between his fingers.

"Ah… What are you doing, Sir?" She backed up and stumbled.

Swearing, he dumped the water and reached for her, grabbing her upper arms before she fell. "That's better," he said, hauling her against him

"It is. Thank you, Sir."

Michael adjusted his hold, placing one hand above her buttocks, the other in the middle of her back.

"You saved me." She stood on tiptoes to kiss his cheek.

He turned to slant his mouth over hers. Compliant, she yielded, responding by opening her mouth and meeting the thrust of his tongue.

She looped her arms around his neck, and when he ended the kiss, she was smiling. Her lips were swollen. "You look like a sub," he said.

"Looks are deceiving."

But she didn't pull away.

He set her back from him, just a bit, and looked at her breasts, cradling them before capturing each nipple. He rolled each between a thumb and forefinger.

She closed her eyes and moaned.

"Are they tender?"

"Achingly so," she said.

He lowered his head and drew one into his mouth.

"Oh, Sir…"

Holding on tightly to him, she spread her legs and pressed her crotch against his leg. "Only filthy girls hump like that."

"Fine. I'm filthy."

"Mine." He flexed his knee so he could help her brace against his thigh.

"Yum. I like this," she confessed.

He resumed pinching and pulling her nipples, mindful to use a much lighter touch than he had last night. She sighed, lowering herself onto him and rubbing back and forth.

"Do I have permission to come, Sir?"

"Since you asked so nice, yes."

She looked up. A smile ghosted around her lips. Their gazes met for only a moment before she closed her eyes and let him take more of her weight. He couldn't reach her breasts that way and keep her safe, so he reached behind her.

This would have been a much better idea on a firmer surface, preferably where he could lean against something. But it was more fun and much more challenging this way.

She moved faster. He responded by smacking one of her butt cheeks while he grabbed a handful of skin on her back.

"That hurts," she said.

"Do you want me to stop?"

"Are you crazy, Sir?"

He encouraged her as she ground out an orgasm, leaving his leg slightly damp. "You're a hot little subbie," he told her when the last aftershock had subsided and she'd straightened her body.

"Thank you." Her words held no gratitude. She stiffened. "But I don't like that word."

"Deal with it. I'm a Dom. That makes you a sub."

She scowled at him. "One plus one is always two?"

"Depends on your perspective."

"Do you see all females as subs?"

He regarded her. It was an odd conversation to be having while standing in the river, both naked, her juices drying on his thigh. "No. Only ones I'm sexually attracted to and who have the same tastes I do."

"I prefer to be a man's equal."

He frowned. "Who says you're not?"

She raked an unkempt strand of hair back from her face. "Doesn't the word sub imply someone's beneath you?"

"It doesn't have to. To me, it certainly does not. I don't see you as less than me, Sydney." He trod carefully. This discussion suddenly felt fraught with danger, and realisation dawned. If she believed those things, it was no wonder she behaved as a brat, in the BDSM meaning of the word. No wonder she had very carefully drawn lines to keep men at bay and to get her kinky needs met. "The word slave might mean that, to some, but to me, the words slave and sub add to a relationship's dynamic. They don't take away. Being a submissive, even twenty-four-seven, wouldn't invalidate your opinions." He took her shoulders in what he hoped was a reassuring grip. "It sure as hell doesn't diminish you, your value or your contributions in any way."

She wrinkled her nose. "Not convinced, Sir."

"It didn't seem to bother you when you were riding my leg."

"You're right about that. It didn't. But it's because I see you, this, as a scene, nothing more. I get my kink on, get off then I go home."

"You had a bad experience," he guessed.

"I..." She sighed. "Do you ever give up?"

"When I win." He smiled to take the sting out of the words.

"I gained valuable knowledge from my time with Lewis."

"But it taught you, or reinforced the belief, that submission is on par with subservience."

She shook her head. "I learnt what I like and what I don't. I got out quick and unscathed. And now I spend more time doing what I do like." She swept her hand wide. "It's not any different from you owning half the state. We've made different choices. Mine are right for me. And I don't have any hoofed pets."

"How serious were the two of you?"

"He collared me. I was young enough to believe in love and happily ever after."

"You don't anymore?"

"I got tired of being a doormat, of making him dinner so he could come home whenever the hell he wanted while I waited on my knees. It seemed a collar meant I was a glorified servant without a single benefit of a wedding ring. I left with less money than I arrived with and a shit-pile less self-respect."

Sydney's blue eyes were wide, exposing the hurt she normally buried under her don't-give-a-damn attitude. But he saw beneath it, and he appreciated the vulnerability she revealed. He was determined to show her she could trust him with the information.

"A friend found me a jeweller to cut the fucking thing off. I've worked hard to get back my independence. Satisfied now?"

"Thank you," he said.

Her shoulders rolled forward.

He kept his voice modulated, slow and soft. "I'm sorry he was a jerk. Some people are. It's unfair to compare me to him, though. I want you to communicate what you want, what you're willing to do. A relationship, even a D/s—especially a D/s—requires constant nurturing and refinement. But I also think it's more freeing. With fewer societal constraints, there are more opportunities to be authentic. You ask or state—we negotiate."

"But what if you demand something?"

"That's where your safe word and slow word come in. You have all the power, Sydney, if you'd just realise it."

"I don't get to tie you up or spank you or deny your orgasm or stand you in a corner with your nose pressed to the wall."

"You're right."

"So how is that fair?" She pulled away from him.

"Because I don't get to do any of those to you without your permission."

She scowled.

"I've hit a nerve with this conversation," he said. "We're different. I sure as hell wouldn't expect you to do certain things around the ranch that I do. Like move mountains of snow from the roads."

"You have a tractor?"

The excitement and enthusiasm in her voice caught him off guard. "Let me restate that. I wouldn't expect you to move mountains of snow unless you wanted to drive the tractor," he added. Her eyes grew wider. It figured he'd be attracted to a woman who wanted to operate heavy machinery.

He heard a splash, and that was quickly followed by a nudge to the back of his legs. "Chewie."

"Is it safe for her to be in the river?"

"Goats can swim," he told her.

"Seriously?"

"She'll need a bath."

"That counts as one of the things you'd never ask me to do, right?"

"Now you're seeing the benefits of division of labour?"

"You might have convinced me."

The goat's arrival had thankfully shattered the tension that had been growing. One thing wouldn't change—his reluctance to compromise. It hadn't worked in his marriage, and any woman he got involved with in the future would have to know who he was, respect it and agree to it. If she couldn't, it was better to find out early, even if it was painful. "Stay today," he invited. "We have a lot of things to discuss."

"I can't." She shook her head.

He didn't think he heard regret in her tone.

"I have a pile of things to do at home, laundry, packing. I leave town tomorrow. I'll be gone for ten days."

He nodded curtly. "I'd better make you a hearty breakfast before you go."

"You cook?"

"Bacon. And eggs from the ranch's chickens."

"Fresh eggs?"

"I get a few a day."

"And there's more coffee?"

"There is."

She opened her mouth then shut it.

"What?" he asked.

"You don't expect me to do the cooking?"

"As I said, there's a lot for us to discuss. Except for where it makes sense to both of us, I don't believe you should do certain things because you're female. My ex-wife was better at managing the finances than I am, and she was better at business plans and some power tools."

"Power tools?"

"There is a tool shed if you feel the need."

"Not really my thing," she said. "What went wrong with your marriage?"

"When she traded her collar for a wedding ring, she also shifted her expectations about sex. What had been fun was now dirty."

"I like dirty sex."

"Yeah. You do." All he could think of was fucking her hard, using her pussy, her ass, her mouth. "And there, I'm in charge. But, to be clear, I expect you to be a sub, not a servant. I like to cook, to select wine to go with a meal, and before you ask, I have no problem loading the dishwasher, either."

She drew her eyebrows together, and he noticed she'd dropped her hands to her sides, as if no longer feeling the need to protect herself. It was a first step. He welcomed it, breathing easier.

"How are you on laundry?" she asked.

"Your lingerie is safe with me."

"The idea of you hand washing my panties stupefies me."

"It shouldn't. I'll just do it while you're still wearing them."

She swallowed deeply. "You don't play fair."

"Never have."

"I thought cowboys had a code, or something?"

"Not when I want you on your knees."

She rubbed at the goosebumps that appeared on her forearms.

"Let's get you dry," he told her.

He followed her from the river. On the bank, he reached for his shirt. He wadded the material and used it to pat her chest.

"The water didn't cause you much shrinkage, Sir."

"Seems to be a constant condition when you're naked." The sun emerged from behind a cloud and he told her, "Turn around."

She did, and he dried the rest of her body. When he was finished, he gave one cheek a quick pinch.

With a yelp, she faced him.

"Payback for the shrinkage comment," he informed her.

She wrinkled her nose. "I suppose that's fair. And speaking of fair, can I dry you?"

By way of an answer, he offered his shirt.

She rubbed it across his head then shaped his hair with her fingers.

"This one piece likes to curl," she said.

"Bane of my existence."

"I think it's cute."

"I don't like cute," he said, his words all but a growl.

"I do."

He captured her wrist.

"I do, Sir," she said.

"That's better." He released her, despite the lack of contrition in her voice.

She continued to draw the cotton down his chest. She boldly took his now-erect cock and moved it so she could dry the lower part of his stomach. Then she knelt and licked his balls.

"Damn, little sub…"

"Oh. Oops. Seems I caused you to get damp again." Looking up at him, she wiped a fingertip across the slit in his penis. Then she raised the pre-ejaculate to her mouth and licked it off.

It was a good thing she had to leave soon. Otherwise he might not let her go.

She dried his legs. "Turn around and spread your legs."

It took her a long time to dry his backside, even tracing up the insides of his thighs, over his perineum and parting his buttocks to daub them.

"Not sure that part was wet."

"Being thorough, Sir."

"Being a brat," he countered. But he didn't stop her. This kind of brattiness, he liked.

He was aware of the sun beating on his body. He didn't need her to continue, but there was no way in hell he was going to stop her. She placed her hands on his waist and used him for balance as she stood.

She slid the shirt over his shoulders, taking her time. All too soon, she said, "All done."

Michael turned to face her. Damn, she was appealing, with her mussed hair, compact, muscular body and red marks—his—on her skin.

She handed back his shirt. He shook it out, and that snared Chewie's attention. The dwarf goat trotted over. She angled her head, trying to grab it from his hand.

Sydney laughed.

"Always funny when it's my clothes," he observed.

"Definitely, Sir."

They dressed while Chewie kept a wary eye on them.

"She's opportunistic," he warned.

"I gathered that," Sydney replied, hurriedly tying her shoelaces.

He picked up the travel cups, and they walked back to the house side by side. Sydney linked her hands behind her back. He swore there was a bounce in her step, or maybe it was her normal energy level. Chewie trotted ahead of them and kept glancing back. When she approached a big rock, she walked up it, stood on top and looked into the distance.

"You weren't kidding about her climbing."

"You're lucky you didn't find her on one of our vehicles this morning."

"That could cause some damage."

"Mostly she behaves herself."

"Just like me," Sydney replied.

"Right."

Once they neared the house, Chewie went towards the barn. Michael held open the gate for Sydney, and he walked behind her up the path.

It was no wonder he liked having her face down. She was all sex and sass.

"Mind if I take a quick shower, Sir?"

"I'll get another pot of coffee going then I'll be up."

By the time he entered the master suite, she was already dressed, her damp hair curling against her face. He wondered if he'd see her in his bedroom again, and he hoped he would.

"Can I do anything to help with breakfast?" she asked.

"You could set the table. I'm sure you'll find everything you need."

She traced her fingertips across his chest before she went downstairs.

He showered in record time.

When he joined her, she had placed a handful of columbines in a small vase near his placemat, making the table look good. The sight of her leaning across the width to pour orange juice into a glass was even better.

While he fried the bacon, she hopped up and sat on one of the countertops as if she'd been a guest dozens of times.

"I think you should wear an apron," she told him.

"I think you should," he countered, cracking half a dozen eggs into a bowl. "And nothing else."

"Maybe I will… Sometime."

Her words and actions kept him in a constant state of arousal.

He whisked the eggs, adding some milk—sans cream—and tossed in some salt and pepper.

"What are you going to eat?" she teased.

"Healthy appetite?" That didn't surprise him after their evening and this morning's adventures.

"Planning to hit the gym later," she said.

"Do you have a workout bag in your car, too?"

"Prepared for anything, anytime."

"Including your upcoming trip?"

"I'm pretty well always packed," she confessed. "I spend as little time in one place as possible."

"Does your name have something to do with that?"

"Probably. I inherited my parents' love of the world. The story goes that I was conceived in Sydney, Australia. Born in the United States. Spent my first birthday in India. My second in London." She picked a grape from a bowl on the counter and popped it into her mouth. "I think I took my first steps in Geneva. Learned to ski in Utah."

"Varied background."

"My parents were adventurers."

Which explained a lot about her.

"Dad was quite a bit older than Mom, and he'd inherited some money. He worked as a consultant, and that took him all over the world. Mom went with him. They didn't accumulate a lot of worldly goods, believing experiences were more important than things. These grapes are sweet." She took a handful and fed them into her mouth one at a time. "I think I was unexpected—not unwelcome, but not planned. So their philosophy was to throw me in a backpack and keep going. Is that coffee ready yet?"

Apparently she didn't like to talk about herself. "Want me to pour you a cup?"

"You're cooking. I'll get us both one. Assuming you want one."

He nodded.

She slid from the countertop. Unerringly she opened the correct cupboard and pulled out two thick porcelain mugs.

"Do you take sugar in yours? Milk?" she asked.

"Just cream."

"Er, I skimmed the top off the milk and used it already."

"I've been holding out. There's a bottle on the second shelf in the refrigerator."

She opened the door and moved a carton of strawberries out of the way. "Score," she said. "If you can't find this tomorrow, I didn't take it home."

He laughed. "Hand it over, will you?" He dropped a dollop into the eggs.

"Are you trying to entice me to stay?" she asked, narrowing her eyes.

"Would it work?"

Instead of answering, she poured the coffee and doctored it up.

"Perfect," he told her after a test sip. "Thank you." He left the *little sub* off the end of his sentence. To him, it was an endearment. He honoured the fact that she disagreed.

When breakfast was ready, she helped him carry the platters of food to the table.

She snagged a piece of bacon before he could serve it. "It might."

"What might?" He pulled back the chair at the head of the table.

"This kind of breakfast, Sir." She sat next to him. "It might make me accept another invitation."

"I haven't tied you to the fence and whipped you yet, either."

She put down the food, uneaten.

"You gave me the blow job and I gave you the spanking. That was only two of three things we discussed."

"You do know how to treat a girl, Sir."

"I hope you have a good trip," he told her, spooning eggs onto her plate. For the first time, he felt he had the upper hand. Her eyes had opened wide before she had spoken. He'd seen her thinking about it, imagining it. And that was exactly what he wanted.

Chapter Six

"You had a mind-blowing night with a hunky cowboy and you walked away without giving him your phone number? Girl, are you crazy?"

Sydney sighed and threw herself down on the hotel's couch. Leaundra, one of her two best friends, stood near the French doors that led to the patio and an ocean view. She had a glass of wine in hand and wore an expression of wide-eyed shock.

"Dish," said Marleen.

The three of them had shared an apartment in college, and they got together once a year to renew their friendship. None of them had changed much. Sydney was the adventurer. Leaundra loved men, shopping and dining out. She'd said she was only going to school to find a man from a rich background and, senior year, she had.

Marleen, a trial lawyer, was the most successful of them all, at least by worldly goods standards. She filled up a second glass of wine with the cheap pink stuff that came from an oversized bottle with a twist-off lid.

Sydney knew the rosé probably wouldn't be considered wine by connoisseurs, but back then it had been the only thing they could afford. It was sweet and went down easy. They could afford better now, so it was probably more for nostalgic reasons than anything else that they trekked to a liquor store and bought a couple of gallons of this stuff. Their taste, at least in this, hadn't evolved.

She sat up to accept the glass. "I only came to Miami to hear about Leaundra's upcoming wedding plans."

"I haven't turned into a monster yet. I've had enough experience to know what's worth getting my panties in a wad for."

True. Leaundra wasn't thirty yet and this was going to be her third trip down the aisle. At least she'd traded up with each engagement. The rock on her hand tempted Sydney to reach for a pair of sunglasses.

"The worst that has happened to me is his mother dragged me to a cake tasting. One of her friends owns a bakery. But really, green tea flavour for a wedding cake? But I figured what the hell? I've had vanilla with butter cream frosting."

"Last time was red velvet," Marleen added.

"See?" Leaundra added. "I've been traditional and it didn't work. So green tea it is. At least it's better than pineapple."

Marleen and Sydney exchanged glances.

"This is what my life has become," Leaundra added from her perch of four-inch heels. "Please, I beg you, let me live vicariously through you."

Obviously getting no reprieve from that quarter, Sydney turned to Marleen. "You've always got fantastic stories about perverted judges."

"You're not getting out of this," Marleen said. "Later tonight I'll tell you about Judge Samuels and what he was wearing under his robe." She filled her glass and lifted it in mock salute.

Sydney and Leaundra dutifully followed suit. They pretended to clink the glasses together, but all of them moving was too much work.

After a sip, Marleen said, "We want to hear about Mr Tie Me Up, Tie Me Down."

"There's not much to tell. He's not any different from other guys I play with at the Den."

"Well, we like those stories too, right, Lea?"

"Damn straight. And he's the first guy you've gone home with since Lewis."

"He was a loser," Marleen added helpfully. "We should have tattooed a capital L on his forehead while he was asleep."

There was nothing like hanging out with friends she'd known since her late teens.

"So, about Michael," Leaundra prompted.

"Master Michael," she corrected automatically.

"Hmm," Marleen said.

"You went to the Den, right? Was the hunky Gregorio character…?" Lea trailed off. "Is he single?"

"You're getting married."

"Oh. Right. I digress. Gregorio warned Master Michael about you, but he approached you anyway. Brave man. Then you talked?"

She sipped. "Yes."

"And went to his ranch in the middle of nowhere. You spent the night."

Sydney nodded.

"You met his goat. Then he cooked you breakfast. And you left without giving him your phone number."

"Correct."

"You left out the part where you got the welts on the backs of your thighs, chickie. Saw them at the swimming pool."

"You should become a private investigator," Marleen said with a raised brow. "If Jack doesn't work out—"

"John. This one is named John."

"I'll hire you."

"I may take you up on it. Do I need a licence or something?"

Sydney grabbed one of the chocolate chip cookies they'd snagged from the lobby at check-in. They'd split the cost of the room three ways, and that was the only reason she'd been able to afford to stay at such a fancy place. If it weren't for her friends, she'd never pay more than fifty dollars a night for a room.

"So, about the welts," Leaundra prompted.

"We had a small scene outside at the Den to see if we were compatible."

"Outside?"

"He had me bend over a fence."

"*Out*side? Like your pants were down and everything?"

"My dress was lifted up."

"Could other people see?"

"Probably not. It was getting close to dark, and we were away from the main house." But the remembrance of others potentially witnessing her humiliation sent a thrill through her. She hadn't suspected that would be something she'd enjoy, but the more she thought about it, the more she liked it.

She took a bite of the cookie and washed it down with wine. She was sure she felt a toothache coming on from all the sugar. "I liked the way he treated me well enough to agree to go home with him." She held up a hand before Marleen could become overprotective. Over the years, Leaundra had stood on the side lines and encouraged Sydney to do crazy things. Marleen would simply start reciting a list of concerns as long as a legal disclaimer. "Before we left, Master Damien took me aside and told me to call if I needed anything. He offered to come and get me if needed."

"Could he have sent Gregorio?"

Sydney laughed. Leaundra saved every conversation from getting too serious.

"Were you your normal, bratty self?"

"Hey!" Sydney protested.

"I'm sure she was guilty as charged," Marleen added.

"Some friends you two are."

"Chickie, who knows you like we do?"

No one. Neither had judged her lifestyle choices, and they'd both listened to her sob over the phone when the relationship with Lewis had ended. In fact it had been Marleen who'd found the jeweller to cut the silver collar off Sydney's neck.

"So did he try to make you stand in the corner like Lewis did?" Marleen asked.

"Loser," Leaundra added.

"You two should take this show on the road. And it was much worse than that."

"Worse?" Marleen took a seat in an armchair. "What could be worse than a timeout?"

"Orgasm deprivation."

"The beast!" Leaundra put her glass on the mantel and fanned herself. "Seriously?"

"Most men I know are thrilled if they can make me come," Marleen said. "I can't imagine any of them trying to stop the big O from happening."

Sydney finished off the cookie. She rubbed the crumbs from her hands. There was nothing like good friends to cheer you up. "It really sucks," she confessed.

"So then what?" Leaundra said. "He has a ranch. He has to know stuff about ropes."

"He does." She recalled him tying her to his massive bed. Then her wayward brain supplied an image of her being secured to his fence while he used a flogger on her. She still wanted to try that. The man knew her all too well, it seemed. He'd left her wanting more, anticipating something she'd never tried.

"When do we get to the welts part?"

"Those were probably from his belt."

Marleen shuddered. Leaundra did a little dance.

"I want to go to the Den with you."

"You're getting married," Sydney reminded her friend for the second time in less than ten minutes.

"There is that."

"So what went wrong?" Marleen asked, more seriously.

Sydney rolled her glass between her palms. "Nothing."

"Did you have fun?" Leaundra demanded. "Those welts sure make it look like you did."

"Well…yeah."

"But you did everything possible there is to do in one night? There's nothing left? You done used that boy up?"

"Well, maybe not," Sydney admitted.

"Did he put anything up your ass yet?" Leaundra asked.

"Ah…"

"He did! *Damn.* So tell me again why you don't want to see him again? You gonna let some other girl get him?"

Sydney took a big gulp of wine.

Leaundra crossed the room with the grace of a supermodel and pulled up a chair. It was as if the friends were forming a protective half-circle around her.

She took a smaller, fortifying sip then set the glass on the coffee table. "We're a mismatch. He owns two thousand acres of land. I own a suitcase and a ten-year-old vehicle."

"Jeez, Syd, you're acting as if he asked you to marry him," Marleen said.

"What's the point in scening?" Sydney countered. "Nothing can come of it anyway."

"Except a good time, chickie. And you should grab as many of those as you can."

"But he wants me to be a submissive."

"And you just want a good whippin'."

Leaundra told it like it was.

"What does it mean to be a submissive?" Marleen asked. "What does he want from you?"

"You could draw up a contract for her."

Sydney shook her head.

"Does he want the same things Lewis did?"

"Loser," Leaundra muttered.

"Like you to be on your knees when he gets home? With dinner made? And looking like a hooker?"

"Chickie, he wanted a brainless fuck-doll. This Master Michael guy made you breakfast."

Sydney nodded. "True that."

"I'd marry any guy who cooked for me," Leaundra said.

"You're going to," Marleen said.

"See?"

"Honey," Marleen said, leaning forwards, "you spend too much time thinking about the future and worrying."

Sydney scowled at her friends over the rim of her glass.

"Because of a few bad experiences, you think you can't enjoy what *is*," Marleen continued. "You're always looking for the next big thing. What if, just for now, you focused on today? If you see him again and have a good time, great. If you don't dig him, move on. No harm, no foul. But don't throw away the chance for a good time because you got a crazy idea that fucking leads to marriage."

Sydney blinked in shock. She expected something like that to come out of Leaundra's mouth.

"What she said." Leaundra grabbed a cookie then sighed and put it back uneaten. "I got another wedding dress to fit into."

"I don't know if he'll contact me."

"So what if he doesn't? He made it clear he wanted so see you again, so stop worrying about what if. Figure out a way to contact him," Marleen said.

"You could call Gregorio," Leaundra suggested. "Hey, if I'm going to be a PI, maybe I could do it on your behalf."

"You're getting married," Sydney and Marleen said simultaneously.

"There is that." She eyed a chocolate chip cookie. This time, she shrugged and grabbed one.

Thank God the conversation moved on.

"I want to hear about the judge," Leaundra said, after devouring a third cookie.

"You'll never believe it. I didn't. But a clerk, I don't care whether he's reliable or not because the story is so tasty, said the judge is a bicyclist. So it's not all that unusual for him to wear those shorts under his robe, instead of trousers."

"I like tight shorts that show off the important stuff," Leaundra said.

Sydney rolled her eyes.

"Well, evidently, when he took off the robe, he forgot he didn't have shorts on."

"Get *out!*" Leaundra exclaimed.

"And he had on this G-string type of arrangement."

"Type of arrangement?" Sydney prodded.

Marleen's lips quivered as if she was trying to fight back a grin. "Uh...trying to be delicate here. It had a pouch to hold the boys. And the other section was anatomically accommodating. Meaning the material stretches as you grow."

"Do tell," Leaundra encouraged.

"I guess he was filling it out, well, not all that impressively. He said it looked like a lime green worm. I think the clerk is in therapy."

"A cock sock!" Leaundra exclaimed.

Sydney laughed. She'd seen a lot at the Den, but nothing quite like that.

The rest of the evening, they drank, reminisced, laughed and ate all the cookies.

When she fell onto the bed face down, she reached for her phone to shut it off only to find a text message waiting.

It was from the Den, asking for her permission to share her phone number with Master Michael.

He was definitely determined.

She felt wildly, stupidly giddy, and her hand trembled as she typed her answer. He'd gone to some trouble to track her down, and she appreciated it.

It wasn't until the following night that she received a message from a Colorado area code with a number she didn't recognise. She was grinning as she opened it.

There were no words, just a picture…of the stilettos Master Michael had promised he'd buy her to replace the ones his goat had absconded with. The red shoes were positioned on top of a box, and the studs that ran up the heels made her heart miss a beat.

She was astounded, first by the fact that he'd remembered to replace her shoes, and second that he'd gone to the effort of contacting her. She also appreciated that he hadn't called and interrupted her vacation.

As she was looking at the screen, another text came through. This one had a picture of Chewie standing on a rock. There was a sign around her neck. Sydney had to zoom in to read the writing. *Sorry I was baaaaaaaaad.*

Sydney groaned. He had a terrible sense of humour. But it had taken some work and creativity to get the photo. She had no idea how he'd got the four-footed eating machine to stand still for long.

She waited and waited, staring at the screen. Nothing else came through.

* * * *

The next morning, the first thing she did was look at the phone. No texts, calls or emails.

But he'd successfully managed to make sure she would think about him all day, even though she and the girls were going out for lunch then shopping for the wedding.

After a champagne cocktail, they stopped in a high-end lingerie store. While Leaundra looked for a white garter belt and stockings, Sydney found a black pleated micromini latex skirt that would look fabulous with the shoes. She purchased a zip-up bolero jacket made of the same material. It had a thick silver metal zipper and plenty of buckles. The two pieces, with the shoes, ought to get his interest.

"You're looking like a chickie who wants to get some when she gets back to Colorado."

"Change of heart?" Marleen asked.

"We'll see."

Towards the end of the day, she checked her phone. Nothing.

When she carried her purchases to the bedroom, she snapped a picture of her ensemble, added it to a text then sent it to him.

She and the girls took a moonlight stroll along the beach.

When she returned to the hotel, the light was blinking on her cellphone. She entered her password to see his latest message. In it, he'd cleverly merged both of their shots into a single image.

The night before her flight home, he sent a single photo of a flogger hanging from the fence in front of his house.

And it wasn't just any flogger. It was red, the same shade as her new shoes. And, God help her, the same shade as she hoped he would turn her skin.

A shudder chased its way through her body.

Suddenly she wished she didn't have to guide a three-day hike along the Continental Divide when she got home. Damn. He was making it difficult to resist him. She was ready to see him.

She replied that she would be home in four days but wouldn't have cell signal for much of the upcoming time.

He answered that he was looking forward to seeing her whenever it fitted her schedule.

She was at her rented Evergreen condo long enough to wash her clothes then pack for the extended hike.

It turned out that she spent the next few days being somewhat of a glorified cook and pack mule. Her clients were younger than she was and were on their honeymoon. They were focused on each other and three was definitely a crowd. For the first time since she'd cut off her collar to end the relationship with Lewis, she missed the companionship the newlyweds shared.

At night, she knew they were trying to be quiet, but the tent walls were thin and the mountains were otherwise silent. She spent hours tossing and turning on the thin bedroll, wanting Master Michael to dominate her.

Finally, under a cloudy afternoon sky, they returned to their vehicles at the trail head. The couple tipped her a shocking amount of money. The envelope of cash put her in a much better financial position to survive the lean period between the end of summer and fall activities and the beginning of the ski season. She generally led some fall bicycling trips in the mountains to see the aspens turn colour, but after the first good snow, even that ended. Sometimes she headed south and looked for other work, but this money would allow her not to do that, giving her several unexpected weeks of vacation.

She cranked up the music, trying to drown out the idea of having extra time to spend with Master Michael in late fall. After all, she hadn't heard from him in days. And that caused even more crazy thoughts to collide. What if he had gone to the Den last weekend and found someone else to submit to him?

When she got back in cellphone range, she pulled off I-70 at a coffee shop.

The notifications screen was all but bare. Leaundra had left a voicemail with the tentative date of her wedding, a year in the future. She had a handful of emails, including one from the Den with a list of upcoming activities. Unfortunately, since she'd been away, she'd missed last weekend's party for Dominant and rocker Evan C to celebrate the release of his new album.

There was nothing from Master Michael.

With a disappointed sigh, she dropped her purse on the console then headed inside for a latte drizzled with syrup and mocha.

Figuring that Murphy's Law would be at work and that she would have missed his call while she was getting her drink, she picked up her phone.

Still nothing.

She dropped her head against the seat back. Unless it was for business, she rarely called men. Especially Doms.

Her cellphone close by, she drove home.

Back at her condo, she dragged in her backpack and went to toss it on the bed. But the outfit she'd bought in Miami was in the middle of the mattress, waiting. In her haste to meet the newlyweds, she hadn't put it away. Now it seemed to taunt her.

She wanted to wear it for Master Michael.

It seemed the harder she fought to keep him out of her head, the stronger the memories were. It was as if she could feel his belt scorching her skin. The welts that had adorned her buttocks and thighs after her time at the Eagle's Bend Ranch had healed, and she craved new ones.

Tamping down her desires, she dropped the backpack on the floor before hanging up the outfit in her closet and shutting the door.

She unloaded the car and stowed the camping equipment in the garage.

Even after she had spent a ridiculous amount of time in a much-needed warm shower, the damn phone remained silent.

Now what?

A modern, empowered woman would contact him. Even Master Michael had assured her she could be a sub without giving up who she was.

After stalling another hour, she picked up her cellular. She entered his number then hesitated. Her heart thundered ridiculously. She had no idea why a simple telephone call could matter so much, but it did.

Closing her eyes, half hoping she'd get his voicemail, she hit the send button.

"Welcome home, little subbie," he said by way of greeting.

His deep, rich voice melted her from the inside out. She collapsed her shoulders against the refrigerator.

"Glad to be back?"

Colorado was a great base, but she had never considered it home, rather just a place to be while she decided what she wanted to do next. But this time she had been happy to get back to her place, no matter how small and unimaginative it was. She'd told herself it had nothing to do with seeing him again, but she knew she'd been lying to herself. "I am." She paused for a second. It would be easy to fall into conversation, but she understood his rules, even if she chafed at them. When he'd answered the phone, he hadn't called her Sydney, but rather by his nickname that defined their relationship. She responded in kind. "Thank you for asking, Sir. I spent a few days in Miami with my girlfriends from college then I guided a pair of honeymooners on a three-day hike of the Continental Divide. They couldn't wait for me to pitch the tents at night, and it took them a while to get up in the mornings. I had a lot of free time."

"I've had some myself. I occupied myself by looking at those shoes."

"I was thinking about that flogger."

"It was custom-made for you. I have others but I wanted you to be able to endure a long, long beating."

She allowed the refrigerator to take more of her weight. "And it matches the outfit," she said, aiming for a casualness she was nowhere close to feeling.

"Always an added bonus. I'm glad you called."

Her shoulders loosened as tension vanished. How did he always know the right thing to say? "I didn't know if it would be okay."

"Little subbie, I'm on the porch drinking a glass of wine and looking at the fence."

Sydney's heart skipped its next beat.

"I wasn't sure when you'd be back, and I also suspected you needed time to sort through your thoughts. I wasn't going to call you, but I was hoping you'd call me."

So he'd been waiting for her to make the next move. She appreciated that he wasn't trying to crowd her. By calling the Den and getting her contact information, he'd reached out and let her know he was interested in her. How was it possible for him to be such a confident Dom and yet give her so much freedom?

"Did you masturbate while you were gone?"

His question caught her off guard. "Not really." She pushed away from the refrigerator and paced the kitchen floor. "I was too tired when I got to bed in Miami — there's quite a nightlife."

"And on the hike the couple didn't inspire you?"

"That's not the right word. I felt more frustrated than anything."

She heard him swallow a drink.

"Tell me why," he said.

"I wanted to have a real experience, not just a fantasy."

"We can arrange that."

Sydney took a celebratory half-step.

"When are you available?"

She wanted to say now, if not sooner, but she tried to act nonchalant. "I'm fairly flexible at the moment. I have an upcoming mud race."

"You mentioned that."

"It's for charity. But I enter every year anyway. The part where I go under the barbed wire is my favourite."

"I may need to raise the bar on my play with you."

Right now, things seemed perfect. She spun around. Maybe Marleen had been right. She spent so much time thinking about the future that she often robbed the moment of its pleasures. "I have no complaints, Sir. So far."

"I've said before that you like to live on the edge."

She laughed.

"How's tomorrow?" he asked.

Yes. Yes, yes, yes, yes, *yes*. "Sounds good."

"You're welcome here, or I am happy to come to you."

"I'll drive up." Not only did she want the ability to leave when she was ready, but she liked the idea of being tied to the fence as he tried the new flogger. "What time would you like me there?

"How about after lunch? Do you remember the code for the gate? Or if you want to call when you're in Winter Park, I'll meet you somewhere."

"I'll be fine. I remember the combination."

"Would you like me to text directions?"

"That would be great, Sir."

"Bring the new outfit. Oh, and Sydney?"

"Sir?"

"Tonight? Don't masturbate. I want you horny when you get here."

His voice, so masterful, chilled her. She hadn't been thinking about it. Now the idea consumed her.

"Please acknowledge what I said."

"It's been about two weeks."

"Then a few more hours won't matter a bit."

She sighed. "Of course you're right." Just those words gave her an illicit thrill. She insisted she wasn't a sub, but when he spoke to her like that, she felt so undeniably female. Though she didn't want to like it, she responded to it, as if it were the most natural thing possible. "I won't masturbate, Sir."

"That's a good sub."

They spoke in generalities before they rang off. It seemed neither of them had been anxious to end the call.

Her skin seemed to sing with energy. Knowing she had to burn it off or go crazy, she changed into running shorts and shoes then put on a sports bra and lightweight top. Finally, she pulled her hair into a ponytail before exiting the condo.

To warm up her body, she started with a gentle jog down the street before crossing over and heading towards Evergreen Lake.

A path encircled the picturesque forty-acre lake and she entered on the dam side. She zoned out as she turned up the dial on her pace. It didn't take long for her to regulate her breathing and work up a sweat as she neared the Lake House. Sydney hardly noticed the other pedestrians or bicyclists, or the elk and deer grazing in the brush. She startled a rabbit at one point, but that barely distracted her.

Finally, more than twenty minutes later, breathless, she slowed to a walk for the trek back to her place.

She took another shower then fell onto the bed. Since he'd ordered her not to touch herself, there was nothing she wanted to do more.

After tossing and turning for an hour, noticing how needy her pussy felt, she threw back the sheet and climbed out of bed.

She grabbed a blanket and went onto the patio to stare at the sky in her version of meditation. Instead of counting sheep, she counted stars. She got to the high five hundreds before she'd harnessed her thoughts. And in the mid six hundreds she started to drift off. Sometime before dawn she woke up chilled and made her way back inside to bed. And when she reawakened the sun was beating through her window, heating her up.

After frying a couple of eggs, drinking half a pot of coffee and updating her website, suggesting some creative late-summer outings and adding a testimony supplied by the newlyweds, she hit the shower.

The imminent trip to Eagle's Bend Ranch had unnerved her.

Last time, she and Master Michael had spent time at the Den before making the journey to his place. This time, it was daylight. Though she knew his expectations, she was less certain how to behave.

Should she wear her outfit? That seemed a bit much given that she would arrive in the early afternoon. Shorts or jeans seemed too casual. And sandals seemed ridiculously out of place, especially if she needed to manage the gate.

If she were practical, she'd have realised that a trip to a working ranch demanded boots, jeans, even pulling back her hair. But she was going for only one purpose.

With a sigh, she threw a few things in an overnight bag, not that she was planning to stay with him, but because she wanted options as far as her clothing went.

She dressed in a pair of serviceable platform sandals and a knee-length skirt. She wore one of her lightweight summer shirts with a black bra beneath. Her whole body felt sensitised now that she knew she would be seeing him and especially because he'd told her not to touch herself.

When she got behind the wheel and lowered the windows to let out some of the heat, she sent him a text message to let him know she was on her way.

The drive took forever, something more to do with her excitement and anticipation at having her sexual desires fulfilled than the actual miles involved. She was glad the road demanded her full attention. At least it kept her from obsessing.

Mostly.

Views from Berthoud Pass stole her breath, and Winter Park was streaming with visitors. As she navigated the lush green high-mountain valley, she saw occasional clumps of wildflowers.

As she left the main road, her pulse picked up a few extra beats. She knew it wasn't from the altitude, since she hadn't had a single problem when she was standing on top of the Continental Divide.

A man she didn't recognise met her at the gate.

"Michael asked me to keep an eye out for you," the older, weathered man said.

"I appreciate it."

The man swung the gate open, waited for her to drive through, then closed it and secured it before he tipped his straw hat, hopped on his motorised vehicle and took off for the bunkhouse.

Master Michael was waiting near the fence, one boot heel hooked behind him on the lowest rail, with a look so sexy it was probably outlawed in half the world. His ever-present hat was angled slightly forward. His jeans rode low on his slim hips, and his shirtsleeves were folded back to the elbow. He appeared at ease, lord and master of all he surveyed. And right now, he was looking at her. Adrenaline tripped through her.

He pushed away from the fence as she braked to a stop near a tree. He opened the door for her and offered his hand as she exited. She couldn't imagine Lewis ever behaving with such elegant manners. It occurred to her that perhaps she'd judged Master Michael, and maybe a vast variety of Doms, too hastily.

"You look fabulous," he said.

"I..." She pulled her hand away and smoothed her skirt. "Didn't know what to wear."

"This is perfect. You did bring the outfit that's kept me up nights?"

"I wouldn't dare forget it, Sir." Just as vanilla men were quirky and some nicer than others, so, too, were guys in the lifestyle. Maybe it was possible that his concept of her being a submissive was different than Lewis' had been. At any rate, he'd promised a nice whipping. Even if she didn't consider herself a sub, she could go along with him for a while to feel his lash. "It's in the bag."

"I'll grab it," he said. "Anything else?"

"No. Everything I need is in there."

He closed both doors and indicated that she should precede him to the house. She glanced around. "Where's the miniature thief?"

"Chewie is annoying the hands who are checking the fence."

"Better them than me." But she didn't mean it. She had already developed an affection for the miniature-sized goat.

"I'll take your bag upstairs," he said as they entered the house. "Would you like to go with it?"

She laughed. "Was that your subtle way of telling me to change my clothes, Sir?"

"Actually, I was asking if you needed to freshen up. I was going to invite you to join me for a glass of lemonade before I beat your ass."

He pushed the brim of his hat back a little, far enough that she had a better look at his sizzling green eyes.

"But now that you mention it..." He dropped her bag on the kitchen floor. The thud echoed through the open space.

Under his scrutiny, she grew warm.

"What kind of panties are you wearing?"

Oh, yes, he was all Dom. And he would never let her forget it. "Boy shorts, Sir."

"Turn around and show me."

Her heart raced. This part of kink excited her. Maybe he defined it as submission, and so maybe they weren't as far apart on what they wanted as she had feared.

He nodded. "Do it now."

She did as he had ordered and hiked up her skirt.

"Spread your legs," he said. "And grab your ankles."

"Yes, Sir," she whispered. Feeling a bit nervous, she did.

For a long time, he said nothing.

Aware of his scrutiny and wondering what he was thinking, she stood there, trying not to move.

"They may be boy shorts, but they're not quite what I expected."

"These are my favourites," she said. The edges were lacy, making the stretchy material serviceable, but also cute.

"You are a constant surprise to me. The moment I have you figured as a leather and latex woman, you wear something like this."

"Is that okay, Sir?"

"Delightful," he assured her.

His footfalls sounded loud on the floor. Then in a great surprise, he grabbed her panties and yanked them up hard between the crack of her ass.

She gasped at the shock.

"Very nice," he said. "You'll not be going home with your ass looking quite like this," he promised.

"I figured as much, Sir." And she'd been hoping she'd bear a few marks to remember him by.

"Stay in position, subbie." He reached in front of her and took hold of the panty fabric.

He worked the material back and forth between her folds, abrading her cunt. She began to move in time with him.

"You're getting your panties damp, naughty girl."

"Yes, Sir."

He increased the friction, and she began to whimper. Holding onto her ankles became more and more difficult. "Oh, Sir... Sir, Sir, Sir!"

"Did you masturbate?"

"No, Sir. I promise."

"Then this has to feel maddening."

"It does. Very much, Sir."

"How long has it been since you came?"

"It was when I was with you last, Sir.

He all but lifted her from the ground. She squealed.

"You must want an orgasm."

"I do. Please. Please, Sir."

"You're compliant when you think you're going to get what you want. And a vixen when that doesn't happen."

He released her.

Bastard. This was the part of submission she hated. And it had the potential to overwhelm everything else.

"Stay in position."

She drank in a couple of deep breaths to contain her frustration. "I don't like you denying me an orgasm, Sir, particularly when I have done everything you've ordered."

"Stand up and look at me, Sydney."

Her hands trembled as she smoothed down her skirt and turned back to face him. She took a step away from him.

"This is the nature of the struggle between us," he agreed. "You want what you want, not what I want to give."

She scowled.

"Can you surrender to me?"

"Is that rhetorical?" She folded her arms across her chest.

"Maybe this was a mistake," he conceded.

"Sir?"

"If you want to be with someone who'll take you to the edge of pain, instead of someone who's interested in taking you to the limits of your endurance to find out how much you're willing to give in order to have a more sublime experience, then you need a different Dom."

"The last time I was with you, I was satisfied. It wasn't how I normally scene. It was different. Better, in some ways."

"I appreciate every aspect when I'm with a woman," he told her. "But I don't get off on just beating her body. I want her mind. I want her fully engaged. And then, when I beat her, she is engulfed."

She tightened her arms around herself.

"If you can let go of your single-minded focus on reaching the end game and, instead, trust that I will take you where you want to be, I think you could enjoy it. Have you ever experienced subspace?"

"Is that kind of like the chupacabra, Sir?" she asked, referencing the mythological goat-sucking creature.

He laughed, shattering the tension. "So I guess your answer is no. It would take a lot of trust for me to get you there, wouldn't it?"

She'd heard some subs at the Den talk about it in vaunted terms. She figured if it were really a place, it would be on a map. "I think it fits in the same categories as unicorns and vampires."

"What do you believe in?"

"Hard work. The uncertainty of life. Things that are tangible. And the fact you deny me more times than you let me come."

"Some women doubt the existence of multiple orgasms."

"Unless they have the right vibrator or a man with a good technique, they're right."

"Maybe the same is true for subspace."

"Maybe."

"You're not convinced. Have you ever had a runner's high?"

She regarded him.

"Same kind of thing, I'm told. Endorphins flood the systems."

"That happens during an orgasm, Sir."

"I'm sure you're right. It's a chupacabra."

But he'd ignited her imagination, and she was intrigued. What if there was something else she hadn't experienced? She'd never considered setting a goal to reach subspace.

Master Michael seemed to believe it existed. Even if it didn't, could being in a different frame of mind make a scene hotter? What if she wasn't trying to protect herself emotionally? What if she followed someone else's lead?

She was sure he was right about one thing. It would take trust. For her, it would also mean suppressing her desires. And it might take a long fucking time. Patience was not one of her virtues.

"Would you like to use the powder room? I'll leave your bag down here until after you've made a decision."

She nodded.

"If you'd like, you're welcome to join me on the back deck when you're ready. Otherwise, I'm sure Pedro will help you with the gate." He exited the room without touching her. She sighed.

She had wanted to show up, get a flogging followed by a long, hard fuck then take a warm soapy shower. Even the idea of being in his bed, all but trapped by his large body all night, had a certain appeal. But he always seemed to have different ideas than she did.

Damn it and him. She hated ultimatums.

It had been a long drive up here and it made no sense to pick up her belongings and head back.

During the time they'd been apart, she hadn't allowed herself to really remember the reality of what it had meant to be with him. In her head, she'd replayed the scenes where he'd tied her up, spanked her, screwed her. She'd kept all the good memories and buried the rest. Master Michael wasn't nearly the jackass Lewis had been with rules and expectations, but he was a long way from vanilla.

So, did she want this badly enough to agree to his terms?

What was the alternative? Go home, masturbate then wait for the next event at the Den? Contact a Dom on the membership website she belonged to? Go to a munch in Denver and meet some new people? All of them would have rules, as well. And they wouldn't have been vetted through Gregorio or Master Damien, so there was an added physical risk, not that that was all bad.

One thing she knew—Master Michael was respectful. He would make sure she came to no harm. And damn if he wasn't irresistible.

She sighed.

Decision made, she freshened up in the main-level bathroom. It seemed presumptuous to go upstairs to the master bedroom without him.

She splashed water on her face then tucked in her shirt. After straightening her skirt, she adjusted her panties so the material no longer cut into her tender parts.

Satisfied that she looked a little more in control, she joined him on the patio. Wondering what he might say, nerves slammed through her. "May I?"

"Please," he said, standing.

His old-world manners charmed her. It seemed incongruous with a D/s relationship. After she had sat in the chair next to his, he resumed his seat.

"This is a different view than the one you see from the front of the house," she said. "A lot fewer trees. And are those cows out there?"

"Good eye," he said. "The river convinced my grandfather to buy, but Granddad built the house over here so that he could take advantage of all the views, and this has a beauty all its own. May I pour you a glass of lemonade? Homemade. It's a bit too sweet for my tastes, but it's refreshing."

"You really are domesticated."

"I like what I like," he said. He looked at her pointedly.

"I am getting that message loud and clear, Sir."

"Out here, it helps to be resourceful."

"You could have a cook."

"Seems a waste for one person. The few hands are fairly adept at taking care of themselves as well."

She accepted the glass and took a sip. "I like it, Sir. Thank you." She tucked her legs beneath her then looked at him, waiting.

"I can make you an early dinner before you go," he said. "I have some steaks and a fresh salad. I'm happy to simply enjoy your company, if that's your preference."

"Ah… No. Thanks." She leant forwards to put her glass on the small table. They'd stalled long enough on facing this moment. "No offence, but I can have a steak almost anywhere."

"Then…?" He regarded her intently.

"I'd like it if we could still scene, Sir."

"Under my rules?"

"It seems I have no other option, Sir."

"Fair warning, I might not let you come until tomorrow."

She sucked in a breath but continued to meet his gaze. She couldn't gauge how serious he was. "If that pleases you, Sir." Even she was wondering how she had forced those words out of her mouth.

"Perhaps I won't let you orgasm at all."

This time she gritted her teeth. "I hope Sir takes pity on this poor sub."

He laughed. "Jesus, Sydney. Did you find a copy of *The Complete Submissive Manual* in the bathroom?"

"Does such a book exist?"

"Not that I know of, but if it did, that line would be in there. Ah." He tapped his fingers together. "While you were inside, did you call Gregorio and ask for a list of responses to give your Dom when you don't agree with him but don't want to piss him off and be disrespectful?"

"Okay, so maybe it wasn't authentic," she hedged.

He raised his eyebrows in his usual, dominant way. "Maybe?"

"What do you want from me, Sir?" she asked, exasperation oozing out despite her attempt to keep it in check.

"Honesty."

"Fine." She tried again, saying, "I may die unless I come a dozen times, Sir."

"That was much more believable."

"And since you don't want to be responsible for my demise, I suggest we start with an orgasm right away."

"I have two thousand acres I can bury you on."

Her frustration eased. He could be difficult, but she knew where she stood with him. No games or artifice. He'd offered her a nice afternoon and a meal, with no expectations of sex and no hurt feelings. But if she wanted to stay? "I can't win, can I, Sir?"

"Only by admitting defeat."

"You don't ask for much."

"Everything you have to give." He paused a beat, adjusted his hat then added, "And more."

"I…"

"The words you used a moment ago? The sentiment is good. When you can utter them and mean them, then you'll know success."

"How do you know I didn't mean them?"

"Your tone," he said. "At times sarcasm is your primary language."

She winced.

"My guess is you do it to protect yourself."

"Psychoanalysis again, Sir?"

"Not at all. You're just transparent. I take it you're staying? On my terms? Whether or not you have an orgasm?"

"Yes," she said. "Yes, Sir, I am." She had doubts that this could be a spectacular night. But she'd had no better offers. Well, she was realistic enough to admit that that wasn't the only reason she was opting to stay. She was staying because, curse it all, despite her intentions to shield her emotions, she liked him. Even if he frustrated her — and he did — she liked being with him. More than that, she believed he had an inborn streak of kindness, which gave her the confidence to emotionally expose herself more than she had in a handful of years.

When she'd accepted Lewis' collar, she would have said she believed he had her best interests at heart, too. But, she had been much younger and considerably more naïve. Since then, she'd had numerous BDSM interactions. The men she'd played with had also been experienced in the scene, even if they weren't lifestylers. Since their hook-ups had been at the Den and nosy Gregorio was always checking up on her, she'd never had concerns for her safety.

"Let's see how committed you are. Please stand, lift your skirt, bend over and grab your ankles."

She knew where this was going. He wanted to test her by repeating what had happened when she had first arrived. Since he hadn't told her to go inside, she assumed he wanted her half naked, out here on the patio.

Slowly she stood and got into position.

"On second thought, I want your backside facing the other direction."

So anyone who happened to be around could witness her humiliation. "Yes, Sir." She did as he instructed.

He moved behind her and slid a finger beneath the elastic of her panties then between her labia. "Interesting," he said.

"Sir?"

"You've been protesting that you hate the idea of submission, but your pussy is wet. I might think you enjoy verbally sparring, even when you get defeated. Especially then."

"Really, you should give up the psychoanalysis, Sir. You suck at it. There's nothing about the idea of submitting that turns me on."

"I disagree, little subbie."

She tensed at the endearment.

"The correct response is, 'I love it when you call me that, Sir. Yes, I'm your little subbie'."

Sydney cleared her throat, trying to cover the fact that she'd nearly snorted.

He continued to move back and forth until she swayed in time with his touch. "You've got a beautiful body, Sydney."

"Thank you, Sir."

"So responsive." He grasped her underwear in much the same way that he had earlier in the kitchen, see-sawing the material harshly over her clit.

Holding her ankles was nearly impossible as he abraded her pussy. She wanted to stand up, to face him, ride his thigh like she had that one time in the river.

Deftly, he brought her to arousal.

She squeezed her eyes shut, wondering if there was any way she could manage a small orgasm without him knowing it. Could she be quiet and unobtrusive enough to hide it?

Right then, he snapped the elastic waistband of her boy shorts, the tiny prick of pain distracting her from the imminent climax.

"You're close," he said.

"Yes. Yes, Sir." Very. She lifted her heels off the ground, unsure if he would really continue to withhold what she wanted, or whether he was testing her.

"Good." He moved faster.

Her legs began to quake. "Oh, oh, Sir. Oh!"

"Would you like to orgasm?"

"Yes! Please, Sir."

He stopped.

She let out a shaky, vexed sigh. Tears stung the backs of her eyes.

"Good little subbie," he murmured. "You're not arguing with me."

He couldn't possibly have any idea how difficult that was for her.

He caught a handful of her hair at the root. "Stand." Because of the way he held her, it didn't hurt.

He helped her up, but when she would have faced him, he kept his hand next to her scalp, preventing her from moving.

"Kneel."

Again, he was there to help her. One of her shoes came off, so she kicked off the other one as well.

"Legs a little farther apart," he said, releasing his grip on her hair.

She complied. Desperately she wished she could look at him so she could decipher his expression. But she knew his behaviour was intentional.

Her skirt hung askew, and a gentle breeze cooled her heated pussy.

"Thank me."

"For what, Sir?"

"My attentions."

"I didn't—" She shut her mouth. "Thank you, Sir."

"I'm not ready for you to come yet."

"Anything you say, Sir." She was a long way from believing that herself. But the anger she might sometimes feel wasn't there. It was a start, she realised.

He moved around to stand in front of her. His crotch was straight in front of her.

"Suck my dick," he told her.

That she liked to do. She fumbled with his belt, then the fastening on his jeans, and he offered no help, seeming to enjoy watching her struggle.

She finally freed him and greedily took his cockhead into her mouth. She loved the clean taste of him and the slightly musky scent. Something elemental jumped through her veins, like the pulse of time itself.

Since he was already hard, it took no time to get him fully erect. She loved the feeling of power that came with arousing him. This man...

He moved his hips a bit, forcing her to take more of his length. She shifted to get a better angle and he withdrew.

She sat back on her calves and frowned up at him. Was he really going to spend the whole night frustrating her?

"You're a great cocksucker," he said.

His eyelids were partially lowered, and from that she knew that he, too, would prefer they continue.

"I am happy to finish you off, Sir."

"I'd like that, little subbie. Later. There's something unutterably rewarding about being turned on," he said.

"I've been told it's uncomfortable."

"It can be," he agreed.

"So then...?"

"I don't ask you to give anything I'm unwilling to endure."

His response surprised her.

He stroked his cock a few times then readjusted himself, zipped his pants and re-fastened his jeans. "Your new shoes are in the master closet."

"Would you like me to model my new outfit?"

"Later."

"Sir?"

"For now, I'd like to see you only in the shoes. I don't want any article of clothing getting in the way while I whip you."

"Yes...Sir."

He offered his hand, and she took it. When she stood in front of him, he said, "Don't touch yourself."

"Anything you say, Sir." This time, she meant it.

Apparently satisfied, he nodded. "Meet me back out here. You've got three minutes."

Chapter Seven

Michael watched her go. Gregorio and Damien had both been right—she was a challenge. But when he'd called the Den to get her contact information, Damien had reacted favourably, suggesting she might be worth the effort.

The two men interacted with all the Den's members. The house's atmosphere lent itself to intimate discussions, so both men knew something about her. Damien had said he suspected she had a tough outer shell to protect herself. Gregorio believed she acted like a brat so that she could collect more spankings without ever opening herself up emotionally. Her reputation, he'd suggested, was a carefully constructed veneer.

Over the last ten or eleven days, Michael had spent a lot of time thinking about her and wondering about the best way to approach and ensnare her. He'd ordered the flogger and new shoes for her. That may not have been his best idea. The very thought of seeing her in them constantly diverted blood from his brain.

He'd contacted her while she was travelling, but only a few times. He'd wanted her interest piqued, but he hadn't wanted her getting nervous and skittering away.

His work with horses had taught him a few things about patience. Even when he wanted to rush things—especially then—he forced himself to take a mental step back. He'd made plenty of mistakes in his marriage, in regards to his expectations. On the day his divorce had become final, he'd grabbed a long-forgotten bottle of bourbon from the liquor cabinet. As he'd downed his third shot of whisky, he'd vowed never again to compromise.

But that would have been so easy with the delectable and determined Sydney. She wanted him to lick her skin with leather kisses. Nothing sounded more appealing to him, either. But ultimately, giving in was a losing proposition. Unless she was willing to commit herself emotionally, she'd simply get her physical desires met and move on to a new Dom.

If the opposite happened and she stayed, he might end up pissed off that he'd sacrificed what he believed in for the sake of a quick fuck. She meant more to him than that. And, Christ, he wanted to mean more than that to her.

When she'd first arrived this afternoon, his denying her an orgasm had infuriated her. He'd debated what to do, feeling that the decision was an emotional landmine. He'd wanted to relieve and reassure her. But he was determined to be clear about where he stood. If they both didn't operate from the same understanding, they ran the risk of crossing over the lines they'd each drawn to protect their hearts.

Michael had been more relieved than he'd imagined possible when she'd joined him on the patio, looked him in the eye and told him she was more interested in sex than steak. So was he. A girl after his own heart.

A loud squeal rent the air.

Evidently she'd found the shoes.

He grinned, delighted that he'd made her happy. He'd do a lot to hear that from her again.

While she was still inside, he grabbed the flogger and a ball gag from a box he'd put together. He laid both on top of the table.

Last night, he'd spent the better part of an hour cutting rope to the length perfect to secure her to the wooden fence. Now he took all four pieces and placed them side by side.

Earlier, she'd challenged him, telling him she didn't believe in the concept of subspace. Maybe she couldn't conceive of the possibility that she might let go enough to lose control. But if she could reach the stage where she was no longer conscious of anything but a delirious cycle of pleasure and pain, he intended to be the one to take her there.

When she rejoined him, shoulders pulled back, chin angled, blonde hair spilling over her shoulders, his mouth fell open.

He prided himself on the fact that he had a hell of an imagination, but with Sydney it hadn't been nearly wild enough. "That's a hell of a get-up, little subbie." The tall red shoes with metal spikey studs on the heels made her calves appear extraordinarily shapely. The full frontal sight of her nearly did him in.

She'd put a touch of scandalous gloss on her lips, making them appear fuller and more kissable. Her small pink nipples were pebbling beautifully under his scrutiny, and her bare pussy drew his gaze towards the juncture of her thighs. The whole package, including her compact athletic body, made him glad to be male.

"Do you like the shoes, Sir?"

"*Fuck me*," he said.

She grinned saucily. "I think that can be arranged."

Now who was in control? "I'm going to give Chewie an extra carrot tonight," he said. "I'm glad she ate your other pair. But the sight of you in these might have caused me a heart attack." No doubt it *had* shaved several years off his life.

"Do you need me to give you mouth-to-mouth, Sir?"

"Cheeky sub." But he needed something, stat. Maybe a bucket of cold water or a jump into the river. Maybe to jack off so circulation could resume. He severed the connection of their gazes so he could focus on something other than his physical response to her nakedness. "I want you tied to the fence, Sydney."

Her smile became somewhat secretive, and the way she licked her upper lip told him he'd intrigued her even more. "Of course, Sir."

That was the tone he needed from her, honest and compliant. This time, they both wanted the same thing.

"Now?" she asked.

"No. Since you'll be totally tied to the fence, unable to get away, we have a few things to discuss first."

Surprising him, she didn't roll her eyes or otherwise object. Was she realising it would do her no good anyway?

"I'll be using rawhide as rope, instead of easy-release handcuffs. It will take longer to bind you and longer to get you out, especially if you panic."

"I won't panic, Sir. I've been tied before, and I trust you more than I've trusted anyone I've ever played with." Then her gaze lighted on the flogger. "Is that the one you sent me a picture of?"

"Would you like to hold it?"

"Do you mind, Sir?"

"I ordered it for you. It's yours." He picked it up and offered it to her.

"It's beautiful. I love the colour!"

"I thought it might suit you."

She took the hilt and shook it, scattering the thongs. "The strands are thicker than I'm accustomed to seeing."

"It's made from deer hide," he explained. "The pain is meant to be thuddy rather than stingy. I think you'll like it. I'll be able to beat you longer than with the other flogger I have."

"But I'll still get marks, right?"

"Do you want them?" he asked, unclear on what she was hoping for.

"Yes," she said. She met his gaze with her open, readable blue eyes. When she looked at him like that, she had no artifice.

The raw hunger excited him.

"Please," she added.

"I live to serve," he told her.

"Thank you, Sir."

The sincerity in her voice undid him. Whatever struggles they endured, she was worth it.

She offered him back the flogger.

"Uh, is that a gag?" she asked.

"It is."

"For me?"

"Is that a problem?" He watched her reaction. The fact that she'd taken one step away telegraphed her nervousness, but she hadn't refused outright, meaning she wasn't distraught. "We're outside. I want you to be able to completely let go without worrying. Your screams will be muffled, and no one will hear your sobs."

She regarded him without speaking.

"If you don't want to wear it, that's fine with me."

"I…" She didn't finish.

"Tell me your slow word?"

"Turtle."

It was the first time she hadn't broken it into two mocking syllables. Progress. Welcome progress from the bratty sub. "And your safe word?"

"Everest."

"Use either at any time."

She looked up. "I promise."

"Thank you."

"Sir?"

"Nothing matters more to me than your well-being. I don't want to fight you to ensure your safety."

"Right now, I'm fine. Horny."

He raised his eyebrows.

"But fine, Sir. I know you'll give me an orgasm when you feel I've earned it or deserve it."

"Are you being an insolent sub?"

"No, Sir. I'm just being agreeable." She smiled brilliantly. "I understand your confusion."

He frowned. She was far too clever for her own good. And his.

Continuing, he picked up a scrap of fabric that was nestled at the bottom of the box. He extended the remnants of the red cotton bandana towards her. "I want you to hold onto this. Since you'll be gagged, it will take the place of your safe word. Drop it and the scene will immediately pause. I'll remove the gag. If you need to be released from the bondage, I'll see to it right away."

She nodded. "I understand."

"Any questions?"

"Only one, Sir."

He waited.

"Can we freaking get on with it?"

"You do understand that impatience won't get things to move faster?" He held back a grin. She was incorrigible, and he appreciated it. "And it won't earn you a more severe beating?"

"You, Sir, are a spoilsport."

He captured her chin in his hand. "Would you like to be tied up and beaten, or would you prefer to suck my dick all afternoon?"

Although she couldn't move her head, she managed to look down at his waistband purposefully "Either or, Sir."

Christ. So much for being the rule-maker. Or for issuing a pseudo-threat. It seemed he was the one at a constant disadvantage. "I want your back to the fence, now, little subbie." He released her chin.

"Yes, Sir." Despite the ridiculous height of the shoes, she executed a beautiful, flawless pivot and headed down the poured concrete path.

He wouldn't tell her, but it had been recently installed just for this reason. Until a few days ago, the back fenced area had been mostly grass that Chewie kept in check. It was far from manicured, but in this rugged environment, he thought the look worked.

He watched the sway of Sydney's hips as she purposefully moved to the fence. Hot damn. If she were his, he'd keep her in those shoes all the time. He'd hire out all the chores, pay a business manager and spend all day playing with her as his sex toy.

The thought was impossible. In winter, she'd need different shoes.

After snatching up the gag, ropes, piece of fabric and flogger, he walked towards her. *That* wasn't easy when all he wanted to do was take her inside and throw her beneath him.

She'd already spread her arms wide and legs apart, and she was watching him, waiting for him.

He had to remind himself he was the big, bad Dom.

Michael kept his gaze focused on her, and she never glanced away. "We'll do the gag last," he informed her.

"Anything you say, Sir."

"You may or may not get to orgasm."

"I..." She opened her mouth for a moment. Resolutely she closed it again. "Yes, Sir."

He raised a brow and waited.

"Whatever pleases you, Sir."

"You sound as if you mean it."

"I do."

His chest constricted. At that moment, he'd have done anything he could to satisfy her. He removed his hat and hung it from a vertical post.

"You can make the littlest things seem so sexy, Sir."

He knelt in front of her and looped the rawhide strips around her right thigh several times before securing her to the fence so that she was looking at him. "How's that?"

"Unyielding, Sir."

"Too uncomfortable?"

"Isn't it supposed to be?"

He shook his head and looked up. "Absolutely not. I don't want you focused on the bondage, I want you surrendered to the moment."

"Honestly, Sir, it feels fine. I would tell you if it didn't. I promise."

Satisfied, he attached her other thigh to the fence. He stood to survey his handiwork. "Are your legs too far apart?"

"It's a little uncomfortable, but not overly so."

"You'll be able to tolerate it?"

"It should be fine, yes."

"Good. I want to be able to hit your cunt."

She pursed her lips before breathing in and exhaling a jagged breath.

"Now your wrists."

He tied her in place then rechecked all the bonds to ensure she was properly affixed. He wanted her secure so she couldn't pull loose and get injured. He also wanted to be sure her circulation would not be compromised.

Satisfied, he took a step back. "Beautiful." And she was. She seemed serene, more so than she generally did. Being tied up suited her.

On some level, he understood that. She could struggle as a physical release. And that gave her tacit permission to let go emotionally. For someone like Sydney, that was probably true freedom. He was glad to go on the journey with her.

Holding up the gag, he returned to her. "Is there anything you need me to know?"

"No, Sir."

"Every part of you is available for me to hit?"

"It is, Sir."

"I will not go near your face or your neck," he said.

"Thank you, Sir. That's thoughtful."

"Are you okay with a ball gag? It's rather large."

"I don't think it's going to look very flattering, Sir."

Wryly, he said, "Other than aesthetically, do you have any issues with being gagged?"

"No, Sir."

"Good. Because I think it's hot when a subbie drools all over the place. Open your mouth." He inserted the ball between her teeth. Since there was only a small part inside he commanded, "Wider." She waited a moment, stalling, but he outlasted her. When she relaxed slightly, he forced it in farther then told her, "Tip your head forwards slightly." Getting her hair out of the way of the buckle was a challenge. "Sorry," he said when he accidentally pulled a few strands.

"'s all right," she mumbled, or at least that's what he thought she'd said.

He adjusted the fit so the straps wouldn't slip. Now it was perfect. She wouldn't be able to properly form any words, and cries would be stifled. "Damn, you are a sexy woman, Sydney."

She blinked at him. Normally he'd like her mouth to be free, but it really was a turn-on seeing that big thing forcing her jaw apart. "Do I need to adjust anything?"

She shook her head.

He grabbed the scrap of fabric and pressed it to her right palm. She closed her hand around it.

He picked up the flogger and shook it out, much like she had done earlier, only he did it with more of a snap to his wrist so the strands jumped. "Your entire body is mine."

She nodded.

He trailed the leather strands across her shoulders, then between her breasts.

She shuddered a little.

"I'm going to give you some time to get used to it. I will warm up your body with a number of strokes before increasing the pressure. I know you want some welts. I'll try to make sure you get them, but I also don't want you bruised or too sore for me to use you in other ways."

Her breathing increased. And when he ran his hand over her pussy, he found she was already slick. "Nice," he said. He masturbated her with his fingers for a few moments then dragged the hilt of the flogger over her clit. She jerked, straining against the ropes.

He kept his gaze on her, tuning into her breathing and her expressions. It was as if the rest of the world fell away.

Michael put the end of the dampened flogger against her vagina. "That's it. Fuck it, little subbie." He held it still and reached around her to give her buttocks some support while she tried to work it inside her.

By wriggling, she took a small amount of the handle.

He eased it out then put it in a little farther. "Shall I use it like a dildo?"

She nodded and tried to speak, but the sound was garbled.

"This is a very pretty pussy, Sydney," he told her while he crouched in front of her.

She moaned.

"Right now, this moment, whose is it?"

Silently she thrust her pelvis towards him.

In reward, he gave her more of the handle as he looked up at her. Her breasts were lovely, the nipples extraordinarily hard. Her legs quivered, and her eyes were luminous with their pleading.

He leaned in and licked her clit. To her credit, she didn't try to sneak in an orgasm, though she probably was figuring she could get away with it because she couldn't ask permission.

Michael was careful with her, being certain she didn't come from his tongue and ensuring she was lubricated enough to accept the handle.

Once he had it in, he licked her faster and faster as he filled her.

Her body shook from silent sobs. He'd be willing to bet she'd never wanted an orgasm like she wanted one now. Earlier, she'd believed she needed one. He was intent on making it worth her wait. "That's my girl," he told her. "Hold off. Do it for me."

She went rigid and she sucked in her stomach. Obviously she was fighting off the orgasm because he wanted her to.

He pulled out the flogger and moved his head away.

When he stood, her eyes were closed. He smoothed a fingertip over her cheekbone. She looked at him. "Oh, yes. You please me very much, Sydney. Thank you."

The gag couldn't completely muffle her sigh as she relaxed her body. Unlike earlier, her body was soft. He wondered if she had made the decision to stop the constant battle between them. Was she willing to put his demands ahead of her adrenaline-fuelled desires? "Are you ready to continue?"

She nodded.

Gently, he began to use the flogger on her body.

He kept an eye on her as the strands caressed her skin. He wielded the implement with precision, whipping her breasts then moving back so he could catch her nipples with the tips.

She jerked.

He watched for signs of distress, but she still clasped the piece of fabric. Satisfied, he adjusted his stance and continued, using both back and forehand strikes on her body.

As he worked, he saw her relax against the bondage.

He moved back a little farther to get a fuller swing and add a bite to the blows. Sydney made a little sound, like a whimper, but when he looked at her face, there was no pain there. Her forehead was relaxed. She may not have reached subspace yet, but he'd bet she rarely let herself surrender this much during a scene.

For long minutes, he continued the flogging, adding more force at times, occasionally hitting her with the broad side of the lashes, then varying the pace so she would never know where the strands would land, or how hard the impact would be.

Sydney closed her eyes.

He moved it up and down her body, hitting her breasts, wrapping the lashes around her waist, flicking between her legs to sear her pussy.

She pulled against her thigh bonds, but she held onto the fabric.

Realising she was letting go of her resistance, he hit her harder, leaving crisscrossed lines on her flesh.

Her head lolled to the side.

Michael considered asking if she was okay, but she appeared serene, and if she was deep inside herself, he didn't want to bring her out. Caught in the moment with her, he whipped her relentlessly, marvelling at the way she responded, her body swaying as she absorbed the blows.

Damn, she was lovely.

For several more minutes, he continued. Then when he believed she couldn't get any more pleasure, her body reddened with welts below her ribcage, he stopped. He considered giving her an orgasm, but he wanted her to be a little more aware when he took her.

In future, he might make a different choice, but for now, he wanted her full participation.

"You've done well, Sydney," he said, keeping his voice barely above a whisper. If his guess was right, she'd want to mentally remain where she was for a bit longer. "I'm going to start releasing you, and it will take a few minutes." He placed the flogger on top of a post before bending to untie her thighs. His head was near her pelvis and he smelt her heat. Her beautiful body was obviously made for this. His cock, which had been semi-flaccid as he had concentrated, went completely hard.

Red marks marred her skin from where the rawhide had cut into her. He rubbed her thighs, enjoying the pattern it had made.

Reaching behind her, he unbuckled the gag. She didn't react when he had to untangle the metal from her hair. "Open your mouth a bit for me, if you can." He took hold of the ball and eased it from her mouth then put it with the flogger.

Sydney flexed her jaw but kept her eyes closed.

"Almost done." He removed the restraint from her right wrist and massaged her skin. Since she'd yet to speak or interact other than to respond to his one request, he used a normal tone of voice as he asked, "How are you doing? Can you move?"

He dropped the last strip onto the grass, and she slowly brought her right hand to her face to push back strands of hair.

"Hey," he said softly when she opened her eyes.

A tiny smile played at the corners of her lips. She blinked, looking as if she were waking up from a drugged sleep.

"I'm going to carry you to the patio," he told her. He swept her from her feet. She turned her head into his shoulder, and he loved the feel of her hair on his cheek and her feminine curves against his body.

He managed to sit while still holding onto her, and he leant forwards for a half-finished glass of lemonade. "Can you drink a little of this?" he asked, offering her the glass.

She accepted and took a few sips.

When he put down the glass, she snuggled against him. He soothed her hair and held onto her, saying nothing and luxuriating in the feel of her.

"That was…"

He waited.

"Sensational. I had no idea. You can do that to me any time."

If she was willing, he had a number of other things in mind to do with her.

After a couple of minutes, she squirmed a bit and looked up at him. "I'm…" She left the sentence unfinished.

"You're what?"

"Nothing. Never mind. I don't want to overstep my bounds, Sir."

"Say whatever you want, Sydney. Always."

"I'm horny. But I'm content to wait as long as you say, Sir. I think I understand more now, about what you were talking about earlier. I didn't get it, but now…"

"Go on." Did she understand? That waiting, longing, subjecting herself to his dominance could transform her experience? Had she learnt that he could be trusted to nurture and care for her, that all her deepest desires would be met and that all men were not like the ass who'd collared her?

"I'm trying here," she said. "I want to be a good sub for you, and I don't want to seem ungrateful."

"I'm listening," he assured her.

"It's not about the orgasm. I don't know. I'm struggling to express what I feel." She curled one hand into a fist. "I want you in me. The connection."

"I don't want to rush you. This is the first time we've played at this level." Hopefully it would not be the last.

"When you're ready, Sir, so am I."

He carried her inside and up to his bedroom. Shockingly her shoes had stayed on, and they aroused him all over again.

Somehow he managed to pull back the comforter and toss the pillows on the floor, and she clung to his neck. He placed her on the bed then grabbed the toy box while she tracked his every movement. He put the box on the nightstand.

She rolled onto her side so she could watch him undress.

"Your cock is hard, Sir."

And had been for days. "You're not the only one who's been deprived, little subbie."

"Seriously?"

"I've told you before that I don't expect anything from you that I'm unwilling to do."

"You haven't jacked off since we were together last?"

"Not even once." Which might have been somewhat of a record for him. He was a sexual man, and he generally started his day by masturbating in the shower.

He donned a condom. As much as he liked it when he'd had her use her mouth to roll it down him, he didn't want to wait that long.

"Shall I keep the shoes on, Sir?"

"Only if you want to drive me wild."

"I'll take that as a yes."

As much as he liked that idea, he looked at them and calculated the damage the spikes might cause his body, especially since he didn't intend to be gentle with her. Those pieces of metal would cause more than erotic pain. "The shoes will have to go for now, no matter how much I'd rather leave them on you." He pulled off one and tossed it in the direction of the closet, wincing when he heard metal connect with the refinished hardwood.

"I guess they're also a weapon, in a pinch," she said.

He removed the second one a bit more respectfully and tucked it under the bed. "Roll on your back and put your feet flat on the mattress," he said. "And let your knees fall to the sides comfortably." When she did, her body was available to him, as if in invitation. "Your body is still red," he told her, tracing some of the marks with his thumb.

"Thank you for doing that for me, Sir."

Oh, yes. She was perfect.

"How are your arms? Shoulders okay?"

"Fine, Sir."

"Good. Then grab the headboard."

She opened her eyes wide and did as he had instructed. It only took him a minute to cuff her in place.

Her breathing increased.

"I'll help you into position, but I want you to put your knees over my shoulders."

He knelt between her legs and lifted her hips since he knew she wouldn't be able to get a lot of leverage herself.

When she was properly positioned, he took his penis in hand and placed his cockhead at her entrance. He captured her gaze and rubbed her clit.

"Sir!"

After her experience outside, he wanted to be sure she really was ready for this. But she rocked her body in silent demand. He'd never been with a woman this free, this voracious. And it stoked his appetites.

He stroked himself as he fed his cock into her. As he surged forwards, his shoulders putting pressure on the backs of her legs, she moaned slightly. "Too much?"

"Stretching my hamstrings and my pussy, Sir. It feels good. Please don't stop."

Now that his cock was buried in her hot cunt, it would take all his resolve to pull out.

"Fuck me," she urged.

That was it.

He placed his hands next to her head so that he could balance his weight. She was obviously in excellent physical condition, but with the angle and the fact that he outweighed her by a good eighty or ninety pounds, he couldn't collapse on top of her, despite the temptation.

After starting with a few long, slow strokes to get her ready, he fucked her hard and deep, jiggling her breasts and making her gasp.

He craved release as much as she did. But this angle, and how incredible it felt, lent itself to another idea.

Calling on all his restraint, he pulled out.

"Sir?"

To her credit, she looked at him with a frown of puzzlement, rather than anger. "Give me a moment," he said. "Keep your legs spread, with your feet flat on the mattress."

"You're making me nervous."

"You should be." He pulled out a small glass butt plug from his toy box.

"Ah..."

"Turtle?" he asked, his back to her as he squirted lube all over the smooth egg shape. He turned to face her again.

Instead of answering directly, she said, "Taking your cock in that position is difficult enough, Sir."

"You can use a safe word or a slow word any time you need to." He suspected she wouldn't, even if it was just because of pride. "We had a discussion that first evening at the Den about your limits. You didn't mention it."

She scowled, and she looked utterly adorable.

Since he valued his hide, he didn't say so to her. "I'll make sure you're prepared as I insert it." And he would watch for signs of real discomfort, not just uncertainty.

"I don't suppose it matters that I don't want that up my ass?"

"Not at all. Lift your legs straight up."

It took her so long to obey that he was beginning to doubt she intended to. He sat on the bed, put his back to her leg then leant back a bit, forcing her into a stretch and keeping her in place. Since she was not going to cooperate easily, so he intended to use his power to force her compliance. The angle he'd selected exposed her anal whorl. "This will be easier on you if you open up."

She kept her muscles constricted.

"It's going in, little subbie. Like it or not." He teased the glass between her pussy lips, running the smooth surface back and forth until her clit hardened.

She exerted pressure against him as she wordlessly sought more.

"So, so perfect," he told her. He ran the egg a little lower, teasing her ass.

"I..."

"It's okay to like it," he promised her. "This is barely bigger than my finger, and you took that fine." He placed the end of the egg to her ass then pulled the toy away. Again and again he repeated the motion, but each time he pressed the plug in a little deeper. When he got to the thickest part, she mewled. Tired of her histrionics, he smacked her cunt, hard. He used the distraction to drive it the rest of the way in.

"That's—"

"In. All the way." He looked over his shoulder at her. "Would you like to continue to protest?"

"No, Sir."

He took hold of her legs and placed her feet back on the sheets. "I'll give you a moment to adjust to the feeling.

"It's a little cold, Sir."

"It will warm up." He washed his hands in the master bathroom before returning to her. "Now, if you'd like, you're welcome to come while I fuck you." His cock was still hard, and he hadn't removed the condom.

"I'm not sure I'll be able to with the pressure."

"It may be a while before you have another opportunity. The plug stays."

She wrinkled her nose.

He moved between her legs, manoeuvring her into position, her legs over his shoulders, and pressing his cockhead against her opening.

"Oh!"

He gave her a moment to use one of her words, but when she didn't he pulled back a bit before moving forward again. She was right about how tight it was going to be. As he finally sank all the way into her, she gulped for air. Her channel was damp and slick, and the pressure from the plug was nearly enough to make him come. "Are you okay, little subbie?"

"Fuck, Sir."

His thoughts, exactly.

"I'm... Do me."

Knowing it pleased her, he lowered himself a bit more, and she grunted.

"I've never had someone so deep." She seemed to struggle a bit for breath, but she didn't protest. "You might have convinced me to do more stretching, though," she said.

He kissed the top of her head before fucking her hard, relentlessly impaling her time and again. There was nothing soft or sensuous about it—it was as turbulent as a mountain blizzard.

With every thrust, she cried out, and he had to force himself to think of her pleasure before selfishly taking his own in her hot body.

"I think I'm going to come," she said.

"Come, subbie. All over me."

She used her knees against his shoulders to dig in and raise her pelvis to change his angle.

"Sir!"

He rocked in and out at a frantic pace, and she screamed as her body convulsed. She thrashed and he gritted his teeth long enough to reach up and release her cuffs. Instantly, she grabbed onto the back of his neck as she rocketed through another orgasm. God, he loved pleasing this woman.

Her internal contractions helped drive his climax. He went still, grinding his back teeth together. A hot pulse shot through him as he ejaculated in powerful spurts.

"Sir, Sir!"

He moaned, and he felt her body convulse again. "Come, subbie," he told her as he shuddered once again, the final bit of fluid surging out of him.

Afterwards, breathing hard, he rolled off her and pulled her tight against him.

She didn't protest.

He held her for several minutes, until their breathing had returned to normal.

"That was…"

"Yes?" he asked.

"Spectacular, Sir."

"No worse for wear?"

"Deliciously sore everywhere, Sir."

That, he liked to hear. "I think we need that steak," he said. "After a shower. Let me take out that plug for you."

"Thanks," she said, rolling onto her side to face him. "I'll manage it."

"Embarrassed? After everything we've done."

"That's a little personal, Sir."

"All the more reason for me to do it. On your stomach."

"Uhm…"

"Tur-tle?"

"Damn you. You know I can't use a slow word, Sir."

"Then the sooner we get this over with the better." Before she could argue any further, he flipped her over. "Stick up your ass."

"I'm glad you can't see me blushing."

He spanked her right below the buttocks. "Enough stalling."

She squealed, but offered her ass.

He grasped the base. "Bear down." The pressure of her sphincter eased, and he pulled out the plug. "Not so bad, was it?"

"Says the Dom. You try being the sub."

"I'm clear on the roles," he told her. "And so you should be, as well." Climbing from the bed, he went into the bathroom to cleanse the plug and dispose of his condom.

By the time she joined him, the shower water was warm and steam filled the room. "It appears I marked you," he said.

She looked down at her body. Like he had done, she traced a couple of the more prominent ones.

He entered the shower unit and invited her in.

"Most men don't share their shower." She looked at him.

Once again, he was unexpectedly struck by her bright blue eyes. The orgasm had drained his testicles, but the sight of her naked, wet body and slightly parted lips was enough to knock him in the solar plexus. "I'm not most men," he reminded her.

"That's becoming obvious, Sir."

"Is that a good thing?"

"Scary."

It was for him, as well. He lathered the soap and washed her breasts and stomach before moving his hand between her legs. "Turn around," he instructed, washing her back and shoulders.

She braced her palms on the tiles, surrendering to his ministrations.

He crouched to cleanse her buttocks and legs.

"Thank you, Sir," she said when he detached the showerhead to rinse her off. "That feels so good. My muscles were a little more cramped than I thought after being tied up. I could stay here all day."

"I'd let you," he said.

He reached for one of the towels he'd tossed over the glass door and offered it to her as he helped her out of the enclosure. "I'll be right with you," he said.

He joined her a few minutes later in the bedroom.

"Uh, I wasn't sure what to put on," she said. The bath towel was still wrapped around her. She had obviously run downstairs to retrieve her bag, but she'd taken nothing from it. When she glanced at him, he saw a tiny furrow on her forehead.

He understood the depth of her question, and he recognised this was another of those pivotal moments. He could tell her to put on the outfit she'd bought in Miami. Or he could tell her to wear the clothes she'd had on earlier. Either way, she was looking to him to define the relationship and asking if he wanted her to stay longer. That she hadn't made the decision for herself told him she was uncertain, too. "I want you to be comfortable," he said, drying his hair with a towel, aiming for casualness he was suddenly nowhere near feeling. "But make no mistake. It doesn't matter what you wear. It won't stop me from fucking you senseless on the kitchen table after dinner."

Chapter Eight

Sydney exhaled a breath she hadn't realised she'd been holding. How did he always freaking know the exact right words to say?

Master Michael walked into his closet and when he came out, he was wearing a pair of faded jeans and seen-better-days boots. He'd put on a navy T-shirt that showed off his biceps and made her imagination serve up all kinds of naughty scenarios. Anytime she was nervous, he defused the feeling and lightened the atmosphere.

"I'll start dinner," he said.

She dressed in her skirt and top from earlier. She couldn't find her sandals then remembered she'd left them outside. Since the yard was fenced, her shoes should still be in one piece. Or at least that's what she told herself.

Barefoot, she went down the stairs but didn't find Master Michael anywhere. The patio door was open, so she went outside and saw him sitting in the same chair he'd occupied earlier.

"Steaks are marinating," he told her. "I poured you a glass of wine."

She sat and accepted the glass.

"I hope red's okay with you," he said. "If not, there's a Chardonnay in the refrigerator."

She had a feeling this wasn't going to be like drinking the fermented fruit juice she had with her friends. "It's fine. Thank you…"

He looked at her expectantly.

She understood. He expected her to use formalities, even if they were not in the bedroom. That chafed, but at least he was clear in his expectations. "Thank you, Sir."

She took a sip and found it to be rich and full-bodied, definitely not like the wines that came out of a jug. Probably it was an acquired taste. At least she wouldn't be tempted to have a second glass, even if he offered one, something she doubted he would.

"Is it acceptable?"

"I bet the bottle has a cork, even."

He frowned, as if he had no idea whether or not she was joking.

"I like it. I think."

"I can get you something else," he said, standing.

"No, Sir. Really. I was teasing." She leaned over to grab the shoe she saw sticking out from under her chair. But she didn't see the match. "Where's my other shoe?"

"Crap." He helped her look before giving up and glancing towards the barn. "The gate was open when I came out. Were they expensive?"

She smiled. "Very, Sir."

"I may have to get a second job. Or a new pet. If my nieces wouldn't be devastated, I'd give her away.

Maybe I should get her a companion? Breed her, maybe get some goat milk?"

"There'd be more of them?" she asked, pretending to be aghast. Then she shrugged. "I *have* been thinking about a new wardrobe. I could accidentally leave out all my things, one at a time."

"You may not like all my replacements."

"You did pretty well on the shoes."

He took another drink of his wine before standing to light the grill. "Would you like to eat out here? That way we can use the kitchen table for fucking."

Her mouth dried.

After dinner, she learnt he was serious.

He carried the plates into the kitchen and she followed with the empty wine glasses. He took them from her.

"Go change," he said. "I pretended to be a gentleman through dinner. But my inner Neanderthal says I'm done being polite."

She looked at him.

"Move it, little sub. Now."

"Yes, Sir." He slapped her ass to hurry her along.

Upstairs, she took her time stripping. This time, his use of the words 'little sub' hadn't bothered her as much as it normally did, maybe because she was focused on their imminent sex. All thoughts vanished when she caught sight of her torso in the mirror.

There were a few faint red marks on her skin, most of which, she suspected, would be gone by tomorrow. She could also see small indentations from his ropes. That reminder of being tied to the fence and flogged beyond reason thrilled her.

She paused.

At some point while she'd been outside, bound and gagged, subjected to a dozen strands lashing her body, she had stopped to think.

She blinked, trying to recall all the events. He'd been striking her belly. She'd felt strangely peaceful. They'd made eye contact, then…

Nothing.

She couldn't remember what had happened between then and him telling her to open her mouth so he could remove the gag. She had no idea that she'd been hit hard enough to leave any welts.

Once he'd loosened her arms, he'd swept her from the ground and carried her to a chair. This meant he'd somehow unfastened her legs without her realising it.

Was it possible she'd reached subspace? After insisting such a place didn't exist?

All she knew was that she'd felt groggy, as if she'd been asleep.

The orgasm afterwards, with the plug, had left her speechless. As angry as she'd been, she hated to admit that he'd been right to keep her on edge. When she'd finally come, the sensation had been more intense than any she'd ever had before.

He'd taken her to unexpected, dizzying sexual heights, making her crazy for more. If he could get over his need for her to behave in a submissive manner, she could enjoy a relationship with him. Coming out here, sceneing, having dinner and a glass of wine when she was in town…?

As she shimmied into the skirt and zipped the jacket, she heard him moving around downstairs. He could wield a flogger and a spatula. Could anything be better?

She slipped on the heels then checked her reflection to be sure her hair looked presentable. The only thing missing was a welt or two on her rear. With any luck, Master Michael would soon remedy that oversight.

When she descended the stairs, he was waiting for her near the table, his belt and four strands of rope in hand.

"Christ," he said, eyes darkening a shade. "I knew the outfit was going to be hot, but I had no idea."

"I hope your inner Neanderthal is pleased?"

"Do you want your butt beaten to match your front, or would you like me to just shove my cock in your cunt?"

His words, along with the way he raked his gaze down her body, from her eyes to her shoes, made her shudder. The comment had been bluntly sexual, but his questions sounded serious. He was letting her choose. "If I may, Sir, I want both."

"I was hoping you'd say that." He nodded. "Unzip that jacket. I want your tits flat on the table.

Her pussy moistened.

Like the expert he was, he secured her to the table.

"Those shoes put you in the perfect fucking position."

He dragged her skirt up over her buttocks.

Before she was mentally prepared, he smacked her ass with the leather. She cried out and pulled against the restraints.

"Would you like the gag?"

"I'd rather scream the house down, Sir."

"Suits me," he said.

Unfortunately, he backed off, warming her with a few gentle spanks. "One or two lasting marks are fine," he said. "But since you're not being punished, I don't want your ass black and blue."

"If that pleases you, Sir." Earlier she'd been able to say something along those lines and mean it. She was hoping he couldn't hear the difference in her tone. Since she would soon be taking a couple of college guys on a mountain-biking expedition, she'd love to have a reminder of him every time she sat on the seat.

He finally belted her hard enough that breath whooshed from her lungs. She pulled against the ropes, but he put a strong hand between her shoulder blades and forced her breasts back onto the table.

She lost herself when his actions were this harsh. This treatment was exactly what she hoped to find when she went to the Den. Who know that a gentleman cowboy would be the one to satisfy her?

The strapping continued, and he even caught behind her knees. She roared out her anguish. In reward, he hit her again, harder, in the same spot.

Overwhelmed with pain and gratitude, Sydney started to sob. To his credit, he kept going, the rhythm soothing her and making her pussy wet.

Then she felt his sheathed cock at her entrance. Instead of entering slowly, he parted her and shoved in with a single, impaling stroke.

He put his hand on her nape, immobilising her as he pounded into her.

It stunned her that he was ready for sex so soon after they'd finished, and that it was this rough fulfilled her.

"Come for me, little sub."

Master Michael used her body so completely she was lost. When he reached beneath her to brutally squeeze one of her breasts, she bucked, granting him deeper access, and when he took it, she yelped and orgasmed.

Bracing himself, he moved his hands to her shoulders. He moved in her with short, quick motions until she heard his tell-tale guttural moan, signalling his climax.

He thrust a few more times, with a little less depth, before digging his fingers into her flesh and surging forward in a powerful motion.

She liked this primal, primitive, driving culmination.

He left her tied in the puddle of tears, her thighs sticky.

This, what she had with him, was what she'd been seeking.

Less than a minute later, he returned and pressed a cool cloth against her. Another thing she appreciated about him. "Thank you, Sir," she said.

He untied her and helped her to stand.

"I smeared the finish on your table," she said as he turned her to face him. He'd got dressed, and that made her feel a bit awkward.

"And your mascara. Christ, that's hot."

"Wrecked makeup, Sir?"

"That you let go that much, yes. There's nothing more rewarding than proof of your tears." He traced the tracks with the pads of his thumbs.

For a moment, she wondered if he might kiss her, and she wondered if she would let him if he tried.

He smiled, leant down and softly said, "I'll get you the furniture polish."

She recoiled.

"I'm a man," he said. "I want to see that skirt ride up as you reach across the table to clean it."

"Are you serious, Sir?"

"One hundred per cent. I could clean it myself, but... Nah. No way."

He really expected her to clean up the mess? Evidently, he did. He rested his hips against the counter, and as she worked, he gave a long, slow wolf whistle.

She glanced back at him. "Really? What are you, a teenager?"

He grinned and shrugged. "I may have to get you a French maid's outfit."

"No chance, Sir."

"Was worth a try. What if Chewie—"

"Again, no. This get-up is going home with me, Sir."

They spent a companionable evening outside. "Are you staying?" he asked.

"Do you have any more of that wine, Sir?"

"I'll get you a glass, since we aren't having another scene tonight."

Although that knowledge disappointed her a bit, she supposed they couldn't always be having sex, no matter how much she would prefer it. It would keep the relationship clearer to her.

He'd allowed her to change clothes, and he built a fire out front. In response to Master Michael's wave, Pedro joined them to toast marshmallows. Evidently not to be left out, Chewie trotted over.

Master Michael scratched behind the goat's ears.

A few minutes later, apparently seeking a new diversion, she jumped on top of a big boulder. Sydney watched in fascination as Chewie looked around, bleated, walked down the far side of the rock then trotted around and did the same thing again. The rock was craggy and had to be three feet tall. "What did you feed her?" she asked.

"Shoes?" Master Michael suggested.

She laughed and popped another marshmallow on a long, thin stick. Pedro was telling a story about Master Michael learning to ride a horse, and she was so fascinated she forgot to constantly turn the marshmallow. Seconds later, the confection was in flames.

She pulled it out of the fire and blew on it. The outside was charred, and the inside was a gooey mess. She wasn't sure she'd ever tasted anything better.

After putting the stick down on a rock, she sat back in her chair, sipping her wine and listening intently as Pedro told stories of Master Michael growing up on the ranch.

"Enough of that," Master Michael warned, interrupting what was probably an embellished tale.

"It's okay, *Señor* Michael. Everyone falls off a horse near a—"

"You looking to get fired?"

"Hay," he finished. "A bale of hay."

Both men laughed.

An hour later, with the bag of marshmallows empty and the moon riding high, Pedro said he'd extinguish the fire.

Her compatibility with Master Michael surprised her.

He joined her in the shower, held her tight all night then made breakfast before she left.

* * * *

Over the next few weeks, she kept up her regular life, including the always-challenging mud race, and she visited him a number of times, but they had numerous small disagreements.

So much about him and their time together was fabulous. But at times his expectations threatened to ruin it. She loved new adventures, like being tied to the fence and venturing into the outer edges of subspace. She was even mostly fine with his aftercare, but when he wanted her to behave as if he were her lord and master, making her wait on his sexual whims for her orgasms, she seethed. Other times, he wanted to enjoy her company, look at the stars, take a horse out to watch a sunrise. To her that screamed of relationship, and that threatened her freedom. She'd started to push to keep the focus on sex. But he was making that more difficult.

She'd been in Moab for four days, guiding a family of six on a hiking trip. Never again would she do that in summer, she vowed. She'd pass that business along to a colleague.

Instead of going home, she accepted an invitation to join Master Michael for a dinner. It had been six nights since they'd hooked up, and she was ready to get her kink on. Hot sex, then head for Evergreen and her own bed so she could get ready for her next job.

The drive down the dirt road took forever, and at the gate, she climbed out of the SUV and entered the combination.

She heard a motorised vehicle and looked up to see Pedro making his way towards her.

"I can manage," she called, waving him off.

Each time she visited, she felt more and more at home. For some reason, this time, that bothered her.

While she'd been in Moab, sleeping under the stars since it had been too freaking hot in the tent, she'd wondered what Master Michael was doing. The cooler temperatures of his land beckoned, and an unwelcome part of her craved the peace and solitude he'd created and wanted to share with her.

And that was the crux of her problem.

Her parents had taught her to embrace life, to seize as many opportunities as possible, and there were still a number of things she'd yet to do. She was committed to living her life on her terms, hitting the road when she felt like it, hanging out with the people she wanted to see, working only for clients she enjoyed.

At the time, getting collared by Lewis had seemed like it would be a kick, a relationship with a twist that had appealed to her. It had taken her more time than she would have liked, but now she was proud of the fact that she'd found the courage to walk out with her head held high. As she'd dumped the pieces of her collar, she'd recommitted to her relationship with herself. Her solo trip to the Bahamas where she'd sipped rum and enjoyed the sun had been celebratory and liberating.

It was tempting to consider staying here with Master Michael. But the potential cost—that of forgoing other life experiences—was starting to give her the chills.

She had climbed back in her vehicle and driven through the open gate by the time Pedro arrived. "You should have waited. But you have no patience." He sighed.

This had become a regular disagreement between them. He didn't like her wrestling with the gate's weight and she liked taking care of herself.

"I heard you coming up the road. Go on. I'll close the gate."

She gave him a quick smile. "Thank you."

She parked then opened the back door to get out her bag. This was becoming a habit, arriving at his house after she returned from an expedition. Each time, she had to shove aside all the outdoor gear to dig out her overnight bag which was now filled with sexy clothes instead of the utilitarian garments it used to hold.

Since her arms were full, she bumped her butt against the door to close it.

She was moving towards the house when she was stopped then dragged backwards, all but yanked off her feet while a rope tightened around her upper body.

She screamed.

Before she could lose her balance, strong arms wrapped around her, steadying her. Next to her ear, Master Michael whispered, "Welcome back."

"What the hell?"

He turned her to face him. "You've been lassoed," he explained. "It's the best way to get the attention of a little subbie and remind her who she belongs to."

She wanted to say she belonged to no one, but, damn it, when he looked at her like that, her resistance evaporated. She should get away. Now. But she didn't. "I—"

"Say yes, Master Michael."

"Anything you say, Sir," she compromised. Her heart still raced, but she had to admit she liked his unusual greeting. "That's a hell of a welcome."

"Wait until you see what else I have in mind."

Damn, he made it so difficult to want to walk away.

He was patient while she showered and changed, and when she went downstairs, sashaying into the kitchen on spiky heels while wearing a garter belt, stockings and leather bustier, she had the pleasure of watching his mouth fall open.

"New?" he asked, sliding a glass of light beer onto the counter.

"For you, Sir."

"Thank you," he said. "I missed you."

"I thought about you," she admitted, taking a purposeful step towards him, playing the diva. "I almost masturbated."

"Almost?"

"I didn't." She raised her hands. "Honest, Sir."

"I'd have had to spank you if you had."

"Really? And how would you have done that, Sir?"

"I'd have sat on that chair." He pointed.

"And then, Sir?"

"I'd have taken you over my knee. Like so."

Quicker than she could have imagined, he reached out and snatched her from the ground. He was sitting and had her over his knee in under three seconds, trapping her legs and bringing his hand down on her rear.

She allowed her body to go limp as she surrendered. She wanted this, needed it, wanted him.

He gave her dozens of spanks, blazing across her buttocks and that tender flesh right below the cheeks.

"Thank you, thank you, thank you, Sir."

Before she fully understood what was happening he picked her up again.

"I should go away more often, Sir."

"I think you should never leave."

She was saved from a reply when he sat her on the edge of the table. He forced her legs apart then pressed on her chest, until she was lying on her back. He pulled a condom from his pocket and dropped his jeans.

"Sir has one thing on his mind."

He looked down at her.

His eyes were dark, and a lock of brown hair fell over his forehead. His eyebrows were drawn together in a straight, determined line. He made her shiver with anticipation, and maybe a sprinkle of nerves on top. She'd seen him in a lot of moods, but this one, pulsating sexual energy from the moment she'd arrived, was new.

"Tell me you don't want me to fuck you like you were missed, little subbie."

"Fuck me like you missed me, Sir."

Before entering her, he put on the latex sheath and spanked her pussy half a dozen times, making her moist. She thrashed her head. *Hell.* She wasn't sure what had got into him, but it excited her.

He parted her legs, holding her ankles and dragging her forwards so that her butt was no longer on the table. She hung suspended, having to count on him to keep her safe as he fucked her. That was heady.

Repeatedly, he slammed into her, moving her around, satisfying her. "I want to come, Sir."

"Take it."

She was lost. The pain from the over-the-knee spanking, the slaps to her pussy, the sensation of weightlessness, the trust she had for him and the days without had left her dizzy.

He moved quickly, propping one of her legs with his shoulder. She was still exposed completely to him, and he pushed on her clit.

With choking sobs, she climaxed.

But he didn't seem satisfied. "Give me more," he said.

He continued to stroke and tease as he thrust, driving her to another shuddering orgasm. On and on he went, continuing to hold back as he relentlessly sought everything she had to give.

By the time he ejaculated, her pussy felt raw and tender. A sheen of sweat covered her, and all her muscles quivered. "That was…"

"Worth the wait?" He looked down at her.

His hair was damp, and his breaths were laboured.

"You really did roll out the red carpet, Sir," she said.

It took her a moment to regain her footing after he helped her to stand.

He went into the small bathroom and when he got back, his pants were fastened. He looked respectable, but damn it, still so appealing.

"Would you like to shower while I decant a bottle of wine and finish making dinner, or would you like to be the sous-chef? Watching you dice and chop while dressed like that is definitely intriguing."

"Oh. You did mention dinner. Thanks for that, but I need to get home."

"I see." His eyes turned the colour of iced emeralds, and she felt suddenly chilled. "Thanks for the fuck?" he asked.

She took a step back. "I'm not sure what the issue is, Sir."

"You stopped by for sex."

"And?"

"That might have been okay if we had discussed it first."

"Why would we?" She rubbed at the goosebumps that had suddenly formed on her skin. She'd sensed this was coming. As they spent more time together, he felt he had the right to make more demands of her.

"I beg your pardon. I thought since you spend half your time here that we did have a relationship. Clearly my mistake."

Fuck. They had fallen into a routine of sorts and she loved the hot scenes enough to keep coming back. All of that had set up false expectations.

"I am not interested in anything other than sex with you." She met his gaze then wished she hadn't when she saw the combination of anger and frustration there. There appeared to be underlying hurt too, and that bothered her most. Softly, she said, "I never

202

agreed to be your submissive, or anything else. I thought you knew where I was at." Good sex, even really good sex wasn't worth that to her.

"Don't let me get in your way."

"I… I apologise…" She debated adding the honorific and decided against it. Calling him Sir would confuse them both.

She turned and went up the stairs. He didn't follow. At one time, he would have watched her, maybe even given her a spanking to encourage her along, but not now.

When she came back down, bag in hand, he was nowhere around.

Her heart heavy, wishing they could have exchanged another few words but also, like him, recognising the futility, she walked to the SUV and climbed behind the wheel. When she arrived at the gate, Pedro was there to let her out. Obviously Master Michael had given the man a heads-up. As she drove through the exit and lifted her hand in farewell, she noticed Chewie was close by, grazing on some weeds.

Sydney accelerated and looked in the rear-view mirror until she could no longer see Pedro.

Determinedly, she concentrated on the drive.

And it wasn't until she was back on the interstate that she allowed her emotions to surface. The realisation she may never see him again taught her one thing—the pain she'd seen reflected in his eyes was nothing compared to the sensation that suddenly constricted her throat, making it impossible to breathe.

Chapter Nine

"Call her."

"Who?" Michael looked up from his office computer screen and saw Pedro standing in the doorway.

"*Señorita* Sydney."

He sighed. "I'm busy."

"I knocked."

No doubt. When he worked on a spreadsheet, he had to focus totally. He didn't like numbers, and he often didn't like the results at the bottom of his columns.

Since Pedro wasn't going away, Michael sat back in his chair.

Pedro grasped a slightly chewed hat between his hands. Michael figured he knew the culprit. He still had to replace his best hat, and now Pedro's, too. This could get expensive. "What?" he asked the trusted ranch hand. Apparently the man had something on his mind.

"You're thinking of her."

"Who?"

"*Señorita* Sydney."

No chance. He wasn't a man who obsessed. He accepted reality and got on with life. Ranching could be brutal. Most winters, he lost cattle to the weather. And spring birthing came with its own risks. He'd grieved for his parents and the fact that his sister and her children didn't want anything to do with the land he loved. And he'd survived it all.

The in-your-face, bratty Sydney only wanted a fuck buddy. He could deal with that as well as the fact that what she wanted conflicted with what he demanded.

"You have been driving yourself like a crazy man. You're hardly eating. You're not sleeping much. You're doing my chores." Pedro went silent for a moment. "You're thinking about her."

"Don't you have some work to do?"

"Did you forget everything you learnt working with horses?" With a respectful nod, Pedro left.

Michael picked up a pen and drummed it on the desk.

Sydney had driven away without glancing behind her. Then again, he didn't much like ultimatums, either.

Part of Michael doubted he'd ever hear from her again. But Christ, the sex had been good, even for him. Getting her off gave him a hard-on.

He'd played with plenty of subs through the years, but since his wife, he'd never had one burrow deep beneath his skin like Sydney had.

So what the hell was he going to do?

Pedro had been correct in his observations. Michael had not touched the spreadsheet. He'd simply been staring at it. It hadn't given him any answers yet.

And no matter how he looked, nothing changed.

He dropped the pen and leant back in his chair, propping his hands behind his head.

And he asked himself a question. Why the hell did she matter? She was a sub. He'd met other women at the Den, some he'd had great times with. There was no doubt that the sexual connection between him and Sydney buzzed with as much energy as a mountain lightning storm. It was intense, immediate, scorching.

To him, it was more than just that, though. He enjoyed verbally sparring with her, liked her vibrancy, her passion for freedom. When she was here, going for walks, splashing in the river, incinerating marshmallows, helping with dinner, sitting around a campfire sharing memories, she breathed life into the Eagle's Bend Ranch. He understood how complex she was and respected her enough not to want to change her.

She might believe, honestly believe that sex was all they shared.

But he knew better.

He'd seen her playing with Chewie when she thought no one was looking. Her blue eyes softened with kindness when she spoke to Pedro. On a recent visit, she'd pulled some weeds out of a flower bed while he'd cooked hamburgers on the grill.

Suddenly he understood.

She didn't keep coming back because they had great sex. She liked being here, with him. To her, there could be no greater threat than that.

Sydney had told him about the man who had put a collar on her. While she hadn't shared all the gruesome details, it was clear she'd had to compromise who she was, and she was intent on not letting that happen again.

Funny. The woman spent her life careening from one adventure to another and she refused to discuss her fears with him. She was so determined to protect herself that she didn't see there was another way, a way for her to have it all—fantastic, edgy sex, a submissive relationship, independence and love.

Love?

He surged to his feet and paced to the window.

Love?

Fuck it all.

That was his problem, why he'd been distracted and irritated, why he was working so many long, physical hours. Somewhere along the line, despite his best intentions, he'd fallen in love with her.

He stared into the distance.

He'd come to a number of realisations in a short time. So now what? Was he willing to let her go without trying? Or was he willing to fight for her, for them? If so, how?

Waiting for her to contact him didn't seem to be working.

Pedro had asked if Michael had learnt nothing in his years of working with horses. He had. Patience. He waited for them to come to him, but he often enticed them. Was that what Pedro had meant?

* * * *

It took Michael a full week to come up with a plan.

He grabbed his cellphone and called the Den. Damien was sympathetic to Michael's frustration but, citing privacy issues, he refused to give Michael her address.

"I can call her and ask for permission," Damien offered. "Leave it up to her."

Since she hadn't yet contacted him, she might be afraid Michael planned to show up at her condo. He wanted her to come to him, not turn skittish. "No, don't do that." Michael shook his head. "If I have a package shipped to the Den, will you forward it to her?"

When Damien didn't answer, Michael continued, "Shoes. Nothing nefarious. Chewie ate one of her sandals. It's only right that I replace them."

"That sounds fair," Damien agreed. "Shoes? Just shoes?"

"Shoes."

"Sexy ones?"

"Not this time."

Damien was silent for a moment. "Clever."

"I hope." They chatted a few more minutes. "Ship them overnight or courier them, will you? Bill me for the expenses."

Damien agreed before Michael ended the call.

Enticement.

He went online and spent over an hour searching out the right pair, almost exact replacements for the ones Chewie had destroyed.

Almost a week later, he was in the barn when his cellular signalled an incoming message. A quick glance at the screen confirmed it was from Sydney.

He blinked. The moment of truth. His plan had either worked or failed completely.

There were no words, only a picture of the shoes.

He waited a day before texting her back.

I'd like to see them on you.

Within thirty seconds, she responded.

I'd like to show them to you.

He thought about his response, and he decided not to play fair. He hung a black flogger from a fence post and sent her a picture of it.

I want to feel it on my body.

It was a start. He typed out at least a dozen replies before settling on one.

Terms negotiable.

Two days later, he figured he'd chosen the wrong response.

He told himself that was all right. He'd left her an opening. Maybe he was wrong. Perhaps all she did want was a fuck partner. If so, he was the wrong man.

Michael was paying bills in his office when Pedro called the office phone.

"You have a visitor driving up the road."

"Sydney?" He sat there, staring unseeingly at the computer screen.

"I never changed the gate code."

"Good enough." He grabbed his old hat, placed it on his head then headed outside to meet her.

She braked to a stop in her usual parking spot. He waited at the end of the path, folding his arms, trying to portray a calmness that was in conflict with how he felt.

Finally she looked in his direction and offered a tentative smile.

A moment later, she killed the engine and exited the vehicle.

Then he got a look at her. *Holy fuck him to tears.*

If all she wanted was sex, he might give it to her, forgetting all his resolutions. She wore the sandals he'd sent her and short—scandalously short—shorts that showed off her tanned, shapely legs. A form-fitting T-shirt hugged her upper body.

She'd left her hair free, and she'd skipped the makeup, hiding behind no artifice.

For a second, he considered striding over to her, ripping down her shorts and bending her across the hood of the vehicle. He'd beat her in punishment for the torment she'd put him through before fucking her harder and deeper than he ever had.

She came around the vehicle, then stopped and leant back against the fender.

"Why are you here?" he asked.

"To negotiate your terms." She swallowed.

Whatever nerves he had, it was obvious she battled her own set. "Did you bring a white flag to signal your surrender?"

"No chance, Sir."

Michael exhaled. She'd set the tone with her respect, and with her sass. And more than anything, she was here, and that meant something.

"I went to the Den last weekend."

He gritted his teeth. Since they weren't together, she had a right to do anything she wanted. But, God damn it, he didn't have to like it.

"I didn't find anyone I wanted to play with. Or"—she shrugged—"maybe Gregorio frightened them into staying away."

"So you're here hoping I'll give in and just agree to fuck you?"

"No." Still keeping her distance, she added, "The truth is, I talked with a few Doms. But I didn't have a connection with anyone. Almost any of them would have tied me to a St Andrew's cross, but I didn't want them to. It felt...hollow. The way I feel about you is what makes the sex so good. I realised that after I left. I've spent years making sure I didn't get involved with any man, and you scare the hell out of me, Master Michael."

"Because?" he prompted.

She shaded her eyes with her hand. "Because I care about you. The land. Even your stupid goat."

"Sounds serious."

"That's why I'm here." She dropped her hand again. "Name your terms."

He hated the physical and emotional gulf standing between them. But he was reluctant to cross to her and take her in his arms until they'd talked more. They'd spent far too little time doing that. "I will give you everything you want sexually. But I cannot compromise on the submissive angle. We can discuss what that means."

"I don't want to give up my business."

"I never asked you to."

She scowled. "What?"

"I'd never want you to give up the things you love. A good relationship should add to your life, just like submission does."

She licked her upper lip. "Do you mean that? You don't want to put a collar on me?"

"I didn't say that."

"I think I'm confused."

"Of course I want to collar you, when you're ready. We will make the rules together. I'm a Dominant, not a dictator. And Sydney, you wouldn't be here if you weren't a submissive." He waited while she absorbed the impact of his words. "If you were honest, you'd admit that. It's more than spanking to you. Turning over your well-being to me is part of what thrills you. That's why it didn't work for you at the Den the other day. You want to give more than just your body. And you want to know the gift you offer is received and protected."

She scowled at him. "I can wear your collar and still guide a back country ski trip?" she asked suspiciously.

"Of course."

"Visit my girlfriends every year, somewhere on planet Earth, without you getting jealous or being mad?"

"Sydney, I want you to live the life you want. You can go as often as you want for as long as you need. Just come back here when you're done. Can you work from here?"

He saw her chest rise and fall in short bursts.

"My condo in Evergreen is closer to Denver and the airport, Sir."

"And most of your work is…"

"Up here in the mountains." She sighed. "Yes, I can work from here."

"Those are my terms. You move in here. We discuss the rules and negotiate them when necessary. You wear my collar, eventually. You show me the proper respect."

"I can't behave perfectly, Sir. I'm flawed."

"Then you'll be punished."

Her eyes widened. "Promise?"

"Do you agree to my terms?"

"Anything you say, Sir."

Her words and tone were submissive and respectful. She'd banished the sarcasm she sometimes used when making that statement. He was smart enough to realise he'd only won because he'd made sure she was comfortable and felt cared for.

He closed the physical and metaphoric distance between them. He pulled her away from the car, taking her in his arms and kissing her deeply. She responded, holding nothing back. Generally he had to coax a response from her, but this more than anything showed him, proved to him that she was no longer resistant to a relationship. "Shall I welcome you home, Sydney?"

"Home," she repeated. "Sounds nice." She smiled. "Did you have something specific in mind?"

"Join me in the barn."

"Sir?"

He took her wrist and guided her alongside him. In the distance he saw Pedro walking towards the bunkhouse, obviously to give them privacy.

"This wasn't what I expected, Sir," she said when he had closed the door behind them.

The space was more of a workshop than a barn. He didn't keep animals here—rather it was a large, mostly unfurnished area that he'd outfitted with heating and air conditioning to protect it from the elements.

A pulley hung down from one of the rafters. "I set this up a while ago for you. I was afraid we'd never get to use it."

"Ah. I'm not sure what you have in mind, Sir."

"Access to your entire body as I flog you."

"Oh, Sir."

He released his hold on her. "Please strip and kneel, little subbie."

She didn't hesitate.

He avoided glancing at her while he lowered the hook. If he looked at her, he'd never give her the thrashing she craved. "Come here," he said, finally facing her.

She rose with elegance and grace.

How the hell had he thought he could live without her? "Here's my promise to you, Sydney. I will try my best to be the Dom you need so you can be the sub you want to be."

She shivered.

"I love you," he said.

"You're doing this for me, Sir?"

"For us," he corrected. "I know how newness and adventure appeal to you. Coming up with something creative will keep me sharp."

"I love you, Master Michael."

He secured her wrists together then fastened them to the hook before adjusting the height to keep her on her toes. He hadn't touched her and already he smelt her arousal. "Perfect little pet."

"Yours, Sir."

"Yeah." He pinched one of her nipples brutally hard. "Mine."

She sighed.

"Another time, I'll blindfold you and gag you while we do this. But for now, I want to see your agony. I want to hear your sobs and screams. Hold nothing back."

"Thank you, Sir."

He kissed the top of her head. "What's your safe word?"

"Everest, Sir."

"And slow word?"

"Freaking *tur-tle*." She smiled. "Sir."

"That will earn you a delayed orgasm."

"Yes, Sir," she said, sounding happy. "If that pleases you."

He was besotted enough to lasso the moon for her. He rolled up his shirtsleeves and removed his hat.

"Now, we're getting somewhere, Sir."

He hung it on a hook then picked up a flogger he'd left hanging there.

As she watched, he took a few practice swings. "Open your legs," he said, returning to her.

When she did, he hit her pussy a few times, making her cry out and respond with a flood of moisture. "You've missed this," he said.

"I haven't come once since I left you, Sir."

The knowledge that no one had touched what was his made his cock harden. "Should I let you orgasm?"

"Only if it pleases you, Sir."

Because she had said it and meant it twice, it did please him. He sucked on one of her nipples and fingered her until she jerked against the hook.

"Sir? May I have permission to come?"

"You may."

"Oh God, oh God, thank you."

As he continued to masturbate her, he realised she'd expressed her gratitude before she came. "Oh, you please me," he said.

After she had sobbed out a climax, he began to flog her with easy, gentle strokes. She never protested. Instead, she let her body go limp in total trust.

She'd changed, and he appreciated it.

By measures, he increased the hardness of his hits.

"Thank you, Sir."

He moved around her in a complete circle, marking every part of her body.

After a few initial cries of pain, she closed her eyes. Within moments, her head lolled to the side. "Subspace?" he asked.

She didn't respond.

"Sydney?" He continued to light up her body, hitting her breasts, her cunt, her inner thighs. "Can you hear me?"

Again she was silent, except for the soft, easy sounds of her breathing.

He gave the backs of her thighs some welts, knowing they'd show if she wore the shorts.

When her body was covered in a sheen of sweat, he dropped the flogger and lowered the hook, capturing her in his arms and carrying her over to a chair. He uncapped a nearby bottle of water and pressed it to her lips.

Dutifully, she swallowed.

He held her, stroked her, snuggled her.

Long minutes later, she roused herself. "I think I was gone."

"Chupacabra?"

She touched his cheek. " Okay, Sir. You were right."

"You forgot the *as always* part."

"I'm not that far gone, Sir."

He grabbed her hand and raised it to his lips.

"Fuck me?"

"Yeah. You up for it?"

She nodded.

He stood and placed her in the chair where he'd been sitting. She watched as he stripped and pulled out his wallet to remove a condom he'd stashed for emergencies. Being inside her—now—qualified as one.

"Have I told you how much I like your tattoo?"

"We should get you a matching one."

"Really, Sir? I'd like that."

The idea of her wearing his brand filled him with possessive energy. "I want you on my lap, facing me," he told her. "Stay where you are." He managed it so that he was sitting and she was in the position he wanted.

"I get to be on top, Sir?"

"But not in charge."

She raised herself up on her knees while he guided his sheathed cock to her entrance. Slowly she sank onto him, exhaling in a slow rush while she did.

"Ride me, little subbie."

She placed her arms around his neck. Her hair spilled erotically over him as she worked her pussy up and down his shaft, some of the strokes shallow, others longer. Within moments, he felt her impending climax. "Wait," he told her.

She bit her lower lip, but she did as he said without protest.

He made her complete several dozen more strokes before he relented and said, "Come now."

When she did, her internal convulsions were so powerful that they drove his orgasm.

She collapsed against him. Sated, he hung onto her.

"You're a sexy man, Sir. Thank you." She leant back, and he met her gaze.

"Did you learn your lesson from your punishment, little subbie?"

"That may take some time, Sir."

"We've got plenty of that," he said.

"We do, Sir."

"Dinner and a glass of wine?"

"I don't suppose you have any in a one-gallon jug?"

"Yeah, actually, I do."

She blinked.

"Anything for you, Sydney."

"Even cheap wine?"

He nodded. "Even cheap wine."

She wriggled from his lap and dressed. As he suspected, two nasty welts were obvious below the hem of her shorts.

With a sassy strut, she walked in front of him towards the house.

Now it was their home.

MASTERED

Sierra Cartwright

Before the evening
is out she's...

IN HIS
CUFFS

Mastered: In His Cuffs

Sierra Cartwright

Released September 2013

Excerpt

Chapter One

Finally.

She'd made it.

Maggie smoothed the front of her short leather skirt and followed her friend Vanessa through the front door of the Den.

Music blasted from the back patio and the bass seemed to shake the walls. Half-naked people — men, mostly — were everywhere, and cool air whispered in through open windows.

Gregorio, the Den's caretaker, met them in the foyer.

"Welcome to Ladies' Night," he said. His eyes were dark, and the wink of a silver earring made him resemble a pirate.

"I'm here for the debauchery," Maggie said.

"You've come to the right place," he assured her with a grin.

She'd been looking forward to this outing for over a month. Not only had she spent her lunch hours shopping online for a new outfit and killer shoes, but she'd also purchased a sparkly collar. Every day at five o'clock, she happily slashed through the date on her calendar. The fat, red mark served a dual purpose. It served as a reward for surviving another workday with the insufferable David Tomlinson, and it was a visual reminder that she was closer to a night at the Den, where she would satisfy her deepest cravings.

"Are you planning to scene tonight, Maggie?" Gregorio asked.

She nodded.

"Sex?"

"I won't say no," she said.

"Condoms are provided in all the private rooms. House Monitors also have them. I take it you want to participate as a sub, not a Domme?"

"That's correct." She wondered how he managed to keep up with the particulars of each guest. But then, that was why he ran the place.

"Are you looking to play with a man or a woman?"

"Strictly het," she said.

Several different coloured wristbands lay on a nearby table. Gregorio selected a white one and affixed it to her wrist.

"Switches are in yellow," he continued.

"That's the one I want," Vanessa chimed in.

"Seriously?" Maggie asked.

Vanessa shrugged. "You never know what opportunities might present themselves."

"As always, Dominants have red bands," Gregorio said.

"Got it." Maggie was anxious to start the festivities. She'd been here often enough that she could take

Gregorio's place at the door. But she also knew he wouldn't hurry through the ritual, despite her impatience.

"House Monitors have black bands around their upper arms. House subs have purple ones. Be sure to let someone know if you need help. The Den's safe word is 'halt', use it at any time. Enjoy yourselves."

"I will, for sure," Vanessa said.

Brandy, a woman Maggie knew as a house sub, took their jackets and purses.

Any night here was fabulous, but four times a year, Master Damien and Gregorio went all out for the house's single ladies, providing entertainment, demonstrations, Doms and Dommes, exotic non-alcoholic beverages and the most mouthwatering desserts imaginable. She'd been saving up her calories for over a week with the intention of indulging in all her favourite things. Not that it mattered, really. If she had her way, she'd burn plenty of energy during a BDSM scene or two.

To her, an orgasm was the best of all stress-relievers. And a dozen would make her forget the crappy hell her life had become.

With luck, it would take less than half an hour to find someone to take her to the downstairs dungeon.

She and Vanessa made their way towards the kitchen and looked out of the patio doors. A fire burned in a pit. People in all sorts of outfits, from street clothes to club wear, milled about. A stage had been set up near the back of the paved area where rocker Evan C all but made love to the microphone.

"I'll have a double shot of that deliciousness," Vanessa said against Maggie's ear.

"Evan C?" The musician oozed sex appeal. Tonight he wore an unbuttoned black shirt, and, as always, his trademark white scarf was wrapped around his neck. A recent video of him had gone viral, thanks to a publicity stunt by one of the Den's members. So now Evan C was giving women all over the world heart palpitations.

"I'd let him put his scarf over my headboard," Vanessa said. "But no, I mean the guy standing to the right of the stage. I think he has on a black band."

Since the party attracted so many newbies, Master Damien brought in extra House Monitors — male and female — to ensure everyone's safety, answer questions and even participate in scenes. "I don't know who you're talking about." Her platform shoes added much-needed inches, but that didn't help her see through the crowd any better.

"The man over there." Vanessa pointed. "Near the speaker. Short dark hair. Jeans. No shirt. Can you see him yet?"

"No."

"Wait. I think that's a pair of handcuffs on his belt loop. Damn."

Maggie craned her head.

"Do you need me to lift you up?"

She glared at Vanessa. Vanessa was five inches taller than Maggie and never missed an opportunity to point that out.

"Would you care for a chocolate-covered strawberry?" a server enquired, distracting them.

"Oh, God, yes," Maggie said.

Vanessa and Maggie both turned away from the huge glass windows and towards the hot man standing near them. He was over six feet tall, with long hair she itched to run her fingers through.

She took her time selecting a treat from the silver serving platter. If nothing else, she enjoyed keeping him next to her for an extra few seconds. Not only did he smell of expensive, spicy cologne, but he had on a bow tie and remarkable, shimmery gold pants. His chest was devoid of hair, and his skin glistened as if oiled. Master Damien *definitely* knew how to please his guests.

She chose a strawberry with the most chocolate coating, while Vanessa, in typical fashion, dived in after the biggest piece of fruit.

Where Maggie was deliberate, Vanessa seized every opportunity that came along. The fact they were so different had made the friendship all sorts of interesting over the last eight years. Maggie nibbled at her dessert while Vanessa bit hers in half.

"Another, ladies?" the man offered.

"Could you leave the tray?" Vanessa asked.

"Don't you dare," Maggie countered.

Vanessa picked up two more berries, but Maggie shook her head. The man winked at Maggie before moving off.

"The sexy man I was looking at earlier is gone. You never saw him, did you?"

"Not like it's a loss. There's plenty of them here."

"True enough. But I like handcuffs. So do you, right?"

Maggie nodded. She loved any kind of restraint.

"So, have you seen anyone you're interested in?" Vanessa asked.

After she'd eaten her strawberry, Maggie surveyed the crowd in the kitchen and great room. "I wouldn't mind sceneing with the HM I played with last time, if he's here. He knew his way around my body without a map." The man had flogged her good then sank to his knees and licked her pussy until she couldn't come anymore. "How about you?"

"I'm greedy. I want two men."

"Two?" Maggie hadn't considered trying a ménage, but now...

"It *is* Ladies' Night," Vanessa pointed out.

"So it is."

The music trailed off and enthusiastic applause followed. She wiped her hands on a paper cocktail napkin then joined in.

A few seconds later, Evan C introduced his next song — the single that was accelerating up the charts — then nodded to his band who cranked up the sound.

"Got your kink on?" Vanessa asked.

"Almost." Nerves assailed her, a heady combination of adrenaline and expectation.

They made plans to meet up later at their hotel room in Winter Park. Master Damien had thoughtfully provided a shuttle between the Den and several stops in the nearby tourist town. "If you go home with anyone, send me a text," Maggie said.

"Same for you."

"Yeah. As if."

"Hey, you could shock the world and do something totally out of character."

Maggie rolled her eyes. Ever since her breakup with Samuel, she'd been in a sexual drought. Then again, it had been all but barren while they were together. He'd tried, at least at first. But after several months, he'd got angry with her.

During one of their arguments, he'd shouted that she was insatiable. That wasn't true. She would have been fine if he'd ever tied her to the bed and used her vibrator on her. A spanking once a week would have satisfied her needs. Well...at least she thought it would have. If it was hard enough, the after-effects would remind her of the pain, then the anticipation would have carried her through the remaining days.

Then again, perhaps the more she got, the more she'd want.

But she might not ever know.

She'd never had a relationship that had made it past six months. If she found a man who was demanding in the bedroom, he tended to be an arrogant son of a bitch outside it. If he was considerate about sharing chores, he tended to bore her once the lights were turned down. And two men had insisted it wasn't right to hit a woman. More than once she'd tried to explain the difference between a consensual spanking and striking out in anger. Her words had fallen on deaf ears.

Recently, she'd cancelled all her dating site memberships. She'd given up searching for Mr Right and decided to settle for Mr Right Now.

Because of that, she lived for her forays to the Den, where her desires were encouraged.

She'd learnt to embrace her single status. She didn't have to answer to anyone if she worked late. If she didn't feel like getting out of her pyjamas on a Saturday morning she didn't have to. She could eat ice cream for dinner or skip vacuuming for so long that dust bunnies threatened to strangle her.

And she could play with different Doms all the time. The exhilaration of not knowing what to expect added to her delirium.

"Targets acquired," Vanessa said over her shoulder as she headed towards a group of men in the great room.

Maggie snagged a virgin pina colada from the granite island in the kitchen then joined the crowd on the patio.

She stood to one side and watched a few couples dance in front of the stage. Off to the left, a tall, broad male knelt in front of a woman who wore a red wristband. The image was erotic, but it didn't do much for her. When she was here, she preferred giving up control. At work, she engaged in constant battles with her self-appointed boss and had to be on guard all the time. Letting go and surrendering to her submissive tendencies was critical to her mental health.

"Would you like to dance?"

She turned and smiled at the man who'd approached her. He was tall and lanky, wearing a plaid shirt. At least he'd skipped the pocket protector.

Part of her knew she was being unfair. He had an earnest smile, and she was sure he was a nice man. He had on a red band, but somehow, she didn't see him as a Dom. There was something lacking in his tone, a certain confidence. And his expression was more hopeful than assertive.

She smiled back and waited a few seconds. He continued to look at her, but she had no compulsion to cast her gaze at the ground. She felt no spark of attraction for him. If she was going to bare her body — or at least parts of it — to a stranger, she would choose a man who had a razor-edge of danger about him. For some reason, this guy reminded her of her of Samuel. She couldn't imagine a greater turn-off. "Thanks," she said. "Perhaps another time."

"It was worth a try," he said easily before moving onto the next possibility, a woman who was swaying as she listened to Evan C.

In some ways, Maggie realised, this wasn't much different than a singles' bar. But there were far fewer pretensions. At least sexually.

Maggie took a sip from the cool drink, loving the blend of pineapple, coconut and whipped cream on her tongue. Since it had juice in it, she told herself the beverage was at least somewhat healthy.

She was ready to take a second sip when she saw him.

David Tomlinson.

Her nemesis.

What the hell was he doing here?

Slowly, she lowered her trembling hand.

Fuck.

The main reason she'd come to the Den was to escape him.

He stood near a speaker, arms folded across his bare chest, a black band on his upper arm, short hair spiked, and he was wearing a pair of jeans.

David Tomlinson was a House Monitor? Crap. It wasn't enough that he was here, but he had to have a role of authority.

Then she noticed the handcuffs.

She gawked at the sight.

Was David Tomlinson the man Vanessa had noticed?

If Maggie didn't know him so well, she might agree that he was sexy. But she knew him too well. He manipulated people to his own ends. Sure, he was one of the smartest people she'd ever met, but she'd seen him use that intelligence for nefarious purposes.

She stood there, uncertain what to do. Confront him? Ignore him and hope he didn't see her? Catch the shuttle back to Winter Park?

Immediately, she dismissed the last idea.

She was here to have a good time, and by God, she would enjoy herself.

Ignoring him wasn't her normal style. No way would she spend the entire night skulking around and looking over her shoulder.

That left a confrontation, and really, the only thing that suited her personality.

As if sensing her gaze, he looked at her.

He scowled—a ferocious expression that was all-too familiar. Obviously he was as surprised and as unhappy to see her as she was to see him. Then a sub walked up to him, and he turned his attention to the blonde.

Maggie exhaled a breath she hadn't realised she'd sucked in.

She took another sip of her drink, trying to regroup. She told herself they were both adults. They were both here for their own reasons. They could deal with this.

Determinedly, she went inside and wandered around the living room. A small group was gathered near the fireplace, and the topic of conversation was the Denver Broncos' upcoming preseason schedule.

Near the window, a Dom rested his shoulders on the wall.

Though he wasn't overly tall, he was broad. He had on a T-shirt, revealing his beefy biceps. He could probably wield a flogger for a good long time.

He glanced pointedly at her wrist then back at her.

Her heart rate increased and she tightened her grip on her virgin pina colada. She cast her gaze at the ground, silently signalling both her submissiveness and willingness.

When she raised her head, she was shocked to see him striding away from her, out of the room.

"If you want someone to scene with, I'll take care of you."

The voice froze her from the inside out. Since she heard it all day, every day, she recognised it instantly. Rich and deep, as controlled as it was reviled.

When her heart started to beat again, she swung to face her adversary. She looked a long way up into his deep, dark blue, unfathomable eyes.

His jaw was set, and his arms were folded across his chest.

"Damn you." She scowled. "Did you make him go away?"

"Yes."

"What the hell is wrong with you? Isn't it enough that you ruin every one of my days?"

"I've always wanted to have you over my lap for the good spanking you deserve."

She blinked, for once shocked into silence by his words. Since they'd met, he'd been standoffish. Business was the only thing they'd ever discussed. And he'd harboured thoughts of having his hand on her ass?

"Maybe we should satisfy our mutual desires."

"Not in this lifetime, David."

"Tonight even," he countered.

She laughed, hoping it didn't sound as brittle as it felt. "Even for you, that's an arrogant statement."

"I spent the last few minutes watching your reflection in the glass, Margaret—"

"Maggie," she corrected through gritted teeth.

"Not only do you have on a white wristband," he continued as if she hadn't spoken, "but you lowered your gaze for that Dom."

Her stomach executed a somersault. "Do you know how to mind your own business? Ever?"

"I pay attention to detail."

"There's an understatement." During the first three weeks that he'd taken control of her family's firm, he'd looked at every piece of paper, analysed spreadsheets, sat down with each employee in private, insisted on meeting all of their vendors and reviewed all current customer files. At this point, it seemed he knew as much about World Wide Now as she did.

"For example, I know you're flustered," he continued.

"So you're a psychic in addition to having superior business acumen?" If sarcasm were arsenic, he'd be dead.

"You're thinking about lifting your skirt for me and lowering yourself over my lap. You're wondering if I'll hit you as hard as you need."

"That's insane," she insisted, but now that he'd mentioned it, she couldn't help picturing that very thing.

"You're hoping I'll let you keep your underwear on. And yes, you are wearing panties."

She blinked, stunned. How the hell could he know that?

"If you were as calm as you'd like me to believe, you wouldn't be stabbing the bottom of your glass with your straw."

She froze, not realising she had been betraying her inner turmoil.

This David confounded her.

In typical fashion, his dark hair was spiked and brushed severely back from his broad forehead. His eyebrows were drawn together in an arrogant, masculine slash.

As she'd noticed earlier, he wore a pair of dark denim jeans, but she hadn't seen the scuffed, black motorcycle boots.

Except for his trademark arrogance, he didn't resemble the man she knew from work.

Normally he wore expensive power suits with crisp button-down shirts. The only concession to an occasional casual look was a loosened knot in his requisite red or blue tie.

She'd spent so much time being irritated by him that she'd never really noticed him as a man.

But now…

His shoulders were broad and his waist trim. The black HM band emphasised the size of his arms. Clearly he had a gym membership, and he used it.

David's jeans showed off the size of his thighs in a way dress slacks never could. Heaven help her, she couldn't help but stare at the thick black belt encircling his waist. Add in the cuffs that refracted the overhead light… He made breathing difficult.

"How about it, Maggie?"

She looked up at him. His use of Maggie rather than Margaret had been intentional, as if he knew exactly the effect it would have on her. She would never scene with a man who didn't respect her wishes, and he was proving he would. "What happened to your no fraternising policy?"

Several more people entered the room, and the noise level increased. He took hold of her shoulders and moved her backwards. She didn't protest. How could she with the way oxygen deprivation was suddenly making it impossible to think?

He released his grip, but he'd effectively trapped her in a corner, her back to the wall. The act seemed symbolic of their entire relationship. He was adept at manoeuvring her to suit his wishes.

Six months ago, when he'd decided to acquire World Wide Now for far less money than Maggie believed it was worth, she'd put up a fiery verbal protest. Rather than deal with her directly, David had taken her mother aside.

He'd told Gloria that Maggie's retention was critical to the success of the firm.

In a brilliant strategic move, he'd then called Maggie back into a private meeting and presented a deal that gave him everything he wanted.

If they met his lofty goals, meaning Maggie worked her ass off and brought in sales, her mother would be rewarded with half a million dollars at the end of two years. He hadn't promised Maggie a penny beyond her regular wages, but he'd somehow figured that taking care of her mother was the biggest incentive of all for Maggie.

Her mother had told Maggie she didn't have to accept his terms. Another deal, perhaps a better one, would come along. Together, they'd figure it out.

But once David had shown her the reality of World Wide Now's fiscal picture due to her mother's mismanagement, Maggie had seen no other option. She loved her mother and wanted her to have freedom from the financial struggles she'd always endured.

If he had simply waltzed in as lord and master, Maggie would have flipped him the bird on the way out of the door. But he was far too smart for that. Still, that didn't mean she liked or appreciated his manipulation.

Once she'd nodded, he'd pulled out an employment contract. The bastard had prepared it ahead of time. She had signed her name with short, angry strokes. In corporate speak, she was shackled in golden handcuffs.

And that wasn't much different from the metal pair dangling from his belt loop. Despite her resolve, she kept glancing at them.

He took the glass from her hand and gave it to a passing waiter.

She felt no fear as he leaned towards her, crowding her space. They breathed the same air, and his scent intoxicated her—power, spiced with raw masculine confidence.

"I think we can both agree this is an exception. You wouldn't be doing this to get ahead at work. I wouldn't be forcing you to do it to keep your job. At the office, we'll have the same arrangement we have now," he told her.

"Meaning you'll set my schedule, tell me what to do, organise my life, prioritise my tasks and I'll agree with you."

"Much the same way as it'll be tonight, yes." His smile was predatory.

She shuddered then regretted she'd allowed him the glimpse of her vulnerability. "I have no intention of sceneing with you," she said.

"The choice is always yours. Do you know the club's safe word?" he asked her.

She blinked. "We're not having this conversation."

"Do you know the safe word?" he repeated.

"Of course."

"Then tell me what it is."

She felt as if she was involved in a game whose rules she didn't understand. "Halt."

"If you want me to walk away, say it."

Awareness of him simmered in her, its effects causing a slow heating of her blood. One word would end their discussion. That's what she should want. So why was she still here, feeling tempted? "You don't play fair."

"I like to win," he agreed. His plainly stated words took away any further argument. "You and I both know that in any D/s relationship, the sub has the real power. You get to set the rules and the pace. If I don't agree to your terms, we have no deal." He paused. "In a way, the tables are turned. It seems to me you should relish that after six months."

"It won't be your butt that's being blistered."

"Or legs," he added. "Or shoulders. Or breasts." He leaned in a fraction of an inch closer.

It stunned her how threatened, how on fire she suddenly felt. He'd barely moved, but she was snared.

"Or pussy," he said finally.

She pressed herself harder against the wall, needing its support. "I'm not saying I would ever agree to your insane suggestion..."

"Go on."

"If I did, we wouldn't talk about it at the office."

"What happens here, stays here. It will change nothing about our dynamic at the office, if that's what you're afraid of."

"I'm not afraid of anything, David," she said, her words infused with bravado she was sure he could see through.

Maggie reminded herself she didn't like him. But damn, there was something about his commanding manner that intrigued her. Every day, she watched him in action. When he wanted something, he pursued it with single-minded determination. A very feminine part of her wondered what it would feel like to be the focus of that attention.

"Do you have your own safe word that you prefer?"

"Halt is fine."

"How about a word to slow things down?"

"Eclipse."

He tilted his head to the side.

"I'm more likely to say accelerate," she told him.

"I wouldn't have figured you for an extreme player."

"You think you're a sage, Mr Tomlinson," she said. "But you've misread a few things about me."

"I'll give you that. From the way you behave at the office, I would have taken you for a Domme."

"It might be fun to strap you to a St Andrew's cross," she said, raising one of her waxed eyebrows.

He laughed.

She blinked. During the time she'd known him, she had never heard him laugh. She'd rarely even seen him smile. Was it possible she'd judged him too harshly? Then she recalled the way he'd even provided the ballpoint pen for her to sign the hated employment agreement. "I'll take that as a no, then."

"Not a chance in hell," he affirmed. "The only one feeling a lash will be you. And feel it you will."

Before she could respond to his flat, arrogant statement, he continued, "I assure you I will be very observant about your reactions." He captured her chin and tipped her head back. "I want to know what quickens your pulse. I'll find out what dampens your panties. I want to know all of your erotic sounds and what each means."

She wished she had met him here first, that she'd seen him as an exciting Dom, felt the connection and agreed to scene. But she couldn't pretend their relationship wasn't already laden with hostility and distrust.

"For tonight," he reminded her. "Just tonight. Say yes, Maggie mine."

If she was smart, she'd tell him no. She shouldn't want this, him. But every nerve ending zinged. Desire won the battle over common sense. "Yes." She nodded.

Desire seemed to flare in his eyes, widening them. "Good," he said.

He released her and stepped back.

She was grateful for the physical space. This close, she noticed how male he was, sexy, sensual and threatening.

"Any hard limits?" he asked.

This part of a negotiation was familiar, and she relaxed into it. She was good at asking for what she wanted. "No blood, edgeplay, permanent marks."

"How about formal protocols?"

She'd had enough experience to know that Doms differed on what that meant. But in this setting, since they weren't a couple, she doubted he would ask for anything she'd find objectionable. "If it suits you, I'm okay with it."

"We'll observe some, but I don't require strict adherence. I want you to communicate."

She nodded.

"What are your limits around humiliation?"

"As long as I'm not left alone for long periods, I'm fine."

"I won't leave you alone, ever. If you're suffering for me, I want to watch and enjoy every moment of it."

There was something about the huskiness in his voice—part promise, part threat—that made her tremble. She looked at him. The set of his jaw emphasised the seriousness of his words.

Maggie would have never suspected she'd willingly experience anguish for David Tomlinson, even offer herself to him, but in this moment, there was nothing she wanted more.

"And suffer you will, Maggie," he promised.

About the Author

Sierra Cartwright was born in Manchester, England and raised in Colorado. Moving to the United States was nothing like her young imagination had concocted. She expected to see cowboys everywhere, and a covered wagon or two would have been really nice!

Now she writes novels as untamed as the Rockies, while spending a fair amount of time in Texas...where, it turns out, the Texas Rangers law officers don't ride horses to roundup the bad guys, or have six-shooters strapped to their sexy thighs as she expected. And she's yet to see a poster that says Wanted: Dead or Alive. (Can you tell she has a vivid imagination?)

Sierra wrote her first book at age nine, a fanfic episode of Star Trek when she was fifteen, and she completed her first romance novel at nineteen. She actually kissed William Shatner (Captain Kirk) on the cheek once, and she says that's her biggest claim to fame. Her adventure through the turmoil of trust has taught her that love is the greatest gift. Like her image of the Old West, her writing is untamed, and nothing is off-limits.

She invites you to take a walk on the wild side...but only if you dare.

Sierra Cartwright loves to hear from readers. You can find her contact information, website details and author profile page at http://www.total-e-bound.com.

Total-E-Bound Publishing

www.total-e-bound.com

Take a look at our exciting range of literagasmic™
erotic romance titles and discover pure quality
at Total-E-Bound.

CPSIA information can be obtained
at www.ICGtesting.com
Printed in the USA
LVOW12s1442101017
551898LV00001B/102/P